Entry from Captain Farrell's Personal Diary

17, February, 2376

Two weeks later and most of us are still alive. We lost three men to some fierce animals that resemble Earth's tigers. Unfortunately we are low on both weapons and ammunition. The trouble with the tigers has made the men extremely reluctant to go on scouting expeditions through the forest.

Considering everything, it isn't a bad planet; we could have had worse luck. We have tentatively named our new home Earth II. After we had a small ceremony about the new name, I found some smart aleck had put up a sign: "Earth Too."

Still can't get used to the three moons, or the thirty-hour days, but I will adjust in time. All in all it is a hospitable place—although I still cannot help thinking that Fate has put us here for a reason, and that danger lies ahead for all of us.

The
SAVAGE STARS

Richard Reinsmith

Ace/Stoneshire Books London

To Sue, my little girl

First Publication in the U.S.A. in 1981 by
Tower Publications Inc.

© 1981 Tower Publications

First Ace/Stoneshire Paperback 1983

Printed in the U.K.

1

For many hours he had remained absolutely motionless in the tall grass while the shadows from the three moons performed a strange, slow dance on every side. Twice he had seen women pass across the high, narrow bridges that connected all the towers. One of the women had paused a few moments to gaze at the fields and the forest beyond. Then she had moved on, disappearing through a doorway.

Jed had said that, years ago, while hunting rabbits in the fields, they found a woman's body beneath one of the bridges. There had been strong winds the previous night. No one could decide if the woman had committed suicide by leaping or if the winds had caused her to lose her balance and fall. Whatever the reason, it had been positive proof that the bridges were high enough to kill. He did not know their exact height, but he estimated the distance to be somewhere between two and three hundred feet. The ground was hard and unyielding. Jed and some others had buried the woman in the forest. They had been afraid the Guiders might blame them for her death. It had been a mistake. They should have left the body where it lay.

The windows in her tower were lighted. His heart beat faster when he saw a shadow at one and knew it must be her.

Alicia.

The memories had plagued him night and day. For the price of ten tiger skins the Guiders had allowed him one weekend with Alicia. It had seemed months ago, yet every detail was startlingly clear in his mind. She had sung to him. She had fed him until he felt sated. Then, in the darkness of the night when he was half asleep, she had pressed against him, and he had learned the ultimate joys a woman can give. She was beautiful. She was perfect. She was ecstasy.

Yet the Guiders' price had been high. It had taken him a long time to collect those tiger skins. He was a skilled Hunter, and still one of his spears had missed a tiger's heart, hitting a chestbone instead so squarely that it had skidded neither to one side or the other instead of imbedding fatally in the beast's entrails. The tiger had become the Hunter, and he had been lucky to slash its throat with his knife. The beast had clawed his back and mangled his shoulder with its long, sharp teeth. He would have the scars as long as he lived—a reminder that Hunters lived on the brink of death. He had six new tiger skins in his cave. Four more and he would be given another weekend with Alicia.

His eyes narrowed as he studied the bridge to Alicia's tower. It was the only way, the only route. The windows were too thin to enter. Somehow there must be a way to reach that high bridge.

How?

A hook, he reasoned. A hook of some sort. Strong enough to catch and hold the edge of the railing. A hook with a long, thin rope. If he devised such a thing, then, with practice, he might be able to fling the hook and fasten it at the edge of the railing. He was strong. He was good at scaling a rope. When he visited the Tree People, he climbed the ropes to their tree homes nearly as well as they, with all their years of experience. With practice, he could become as good, no, *better* than they.

Filled with fresh determination, he turned and crawled slowly through the grass until he reached the edge of the forest. Although he was careful and felt sure no one had detected his presence, there was one woman who observed the shadow of his body as it slithered across the ground. With a shudder of horror, she took it to be an enormous snake. Closing and locking the windows on her tower room, she went to bed. Her sleep was filled with nightmares.

The Tree Father was in a good mood. Eric was glad he had come to discuss his plans. It was a beautiful morning, the sky a deep and pure blue as far as the eye could see. A breeze swept across the tree tops and seemed to bring more than the freshness of the thriving forest. Eric thought he could detect a wisp of the cool air down from the mountains.

"I have come to tell you my plans," Eric said as he studied the other's face. The Tree Father was very old, his hair a sparse, frosty cap, his skin covered with an incredible number of wrinkles. His eyes were young and vital, though, fully alive, and sparkling with an intelligence not to be found anywhere else. This was one of the main features that fascinated Eric, and although the older man's skin was very wrinkled Eric had not failed to notice that his movements were always quick and steady.

"Good," the Father said. "I like to hear plans. Shall we smoke?"

Eric nodded affirmatively. He watched silently as the Father filled two pipes with tobacco. When their pipes were lit and they had both luxuriously inhaled and exhaled, he continued, "You may think my plans are foolhardy. You may think I am crazy."

"Oh?"

"I want to steal a woman."

"The one you spent the weekend with?"

"Yes."

"She was your first woman?"

"Yes."

"What was her name?"

"Alicia."

The older man frowned. His forehead was so wrinkled that the frown was not evidenced by the appearance of new lines but by the shifting and deepening of ancient ones. "I do not recall hearing the name before."

"She is young and relatively inexperienced, I think."

"And you wish to steal her. For how long? A

week, a month, a year, to trade for something else?"

Eric could not quite understand his own emotions, but he felt his cheeks redden. "I want to keep her forever after I have stolen her."

"Ah, she pleased you greatly."

Eric nodded again. At times he felt boyish in the Father's presence. This was one of those times. The flush in his cheeks deepened. To hide his coloring, he turned and looked away, out the doorway and across the top of the forest. The Tree Father's house was located on the highest tree of the tallest hill. The view was spectacular in its own way. A person could see many miles in any direction.

"Do you think I'm crazy?" Eric asked.

The Tree Father laughed. "No. When you first said you had a plan that may be considered foolhardy, I thought you might be considering a revolution against the Guiders. To want to steal a woman is a natural ambition. Many young men have come to me and confessed similar desires." He sighed. "In my younger days . . ." He chuckled and the chuckles faded away to silence. Eric waited patiently. After the Father had puffed on his pipe awhile, he shrugged philosophically. "My body is too old for strong desires for women." He raised a wrinkled hand. "Although I must admit I would enjoy the constant company of one. It would be a thing of the mind. I like to see their long hair and soft skin. I enjoy their gentle ways and senseless chatter. It is a special kind of music."

"Then I shall steal one for you too," Eric joked. Having inhaled deeply on the pipe, he felt lightheaded and festive.

The Tree Father nodded his appreciation, although he clearly knew it was a joke. "Tell me, what will you do with this woman after you have stolen her?"

"I have chosen a place in the forest, the place they call the Valley of the Tigers. None of your people go there because they are afraid. I have room in a tree there. She cannot escape, she will be afraid of the tigers also."

"This woman, what did you say her name was?"

"Alicia."

"Yes. Did this Alicia appear to, ah, like your company?"

"I think so. During the night, in the dark, when we were together, she clawed my back. At first I thought it was in anger or pain but then I understood it was in great pleasure."

"Ah." The sound was a soft whisper from the old man's lips. For a long while his eyes were remote as if seeing something far away, perhaps in the distant past.

"I am serious," Eric affirmed. "This is not an idle dream. I will steal her."

"The Guiders will be angry."

"I know."

"And they will send the metal dogs to search for her and you. They will trace her scent. And yours, too, if you have left anything behind for them to recognize. What will you do when the metal dogs come in search? Your spears and knives cannot hurt their tough skin."

"But I have heard they cannot cross a river.

When the sky breaks, they hide from the rain. Someone has said they catch a disease called rust."

"True."

"And the Valley of the Tigers is beyond a river."

"But what if the dogs find a way to cross the river?"

"I shall hope to be on the other side of the river before they reach it. Our scent will be beyond their senses."

"What if things go wrong? What if they reach you before you reach the river?"

"I have thought of that possibility," Eric said grimly.

"Their teeth are sharp."

"I will bash their brains in with a club I have made. I will carry the club in addition to my spear and two knives that I will have when I steal Alicia."

The old man smiled, and it seemed to Eric that there was a new gleam of interest in his gray eyes. "Who told you their brains could be broken with a club?"

"I have been sworn to secrecy."

"I respect your vow. But it would not be breaking your vow if you tell me the details without saying who gave them to you."

Eric hesitated and then decided the man's identity was the only element that needed to be kept secret. "Will you promise not to repeat any of what I say?"

The Tree Father's face was expressionless, but he ran the tips of his fingers across his wrinkled face and through his white hair. "One of the necessities of living to a ripe age is the ability to keep secrets."

Eric cleared his throat. This was something he had never told anyone before, although he had in his mind dwelled on the details numerous times.

"A woman escaped the Castle many years ago. I am sure you have heard the story. It was said that she offended one of the Guiders, although no one knows how. They sent the dogs after her and they killed her. One of your people saw the killing and was greatly angered. It began to rain, and the metal dogs scattered to hide beneath the thick branches of some trees. There were three dogs. When frightened of the rust disease, two hid beneath one tree, but one was alone. The person who told me the story said he descended on a vine until he was near the dog. It appeared to be asleep. The person was carrying a club. He—"

"What kind of club?" the old man interrupted.

"It was a stick about three feet with a rock strapped to the end. He said he had been using it to crack the nuts that grow in the trees with the purple leaves."

"Purple nuts as we call them," The Tree Father said with a sudden smile. "It has been a long time since I have had some. I had a great fondness for purple nuts."

Eric shifted to a different position on the cushion, vaguely annoyed that the conversation had shifted from the important life-and-death matter to the subject of purple nuts. When the old man fell silent again, he continued:

"On an impulse he smashed the club against the dog's head. He heard a cracking as of dry twigs, he said. And the dog fell lifeless. This man knew spears and knives could not pierce a metal dog's skin, but he discovered their brains were fragile.''

"Did you see this particular dog?"

"No."

"Then you have no evidence that your friend was telling the truth?"

"No."

"And yet you have fashioned a club to fight metal dogs?"

"Yes." For the first time since he heard the story, Eric began to doubt its truth.

"Close the door and lock it," the Tree Father said softly. "I want to show you something."

Eric closed the door and slid the latch in place. There were open windows on every side, but they faced the emptiness of space with no danger that anyone would pass by one of them.

The old man motioned toward a round rug near a far wall. "Look beneath the rug."

Bewildered, Eric crossed the room and slowly slid the rug aside. He saw the outline of a door beneath, a door with a recessed handle.

"Open it."

Eric lifted the door. There, in a small compartment, was one of the metal dogs.

Entry in Captain Farrell's personal diary, Feb. 17, 2376:

Two weeks later and most of us are still alive. We lost three men to some animals that resemble earth's tigers. There is some difference in the shape of the head, the body size, and the stripes, but the

13

resemblance is so close that the men have started to refer to them as tigers.

Unfortunately we are low on both weapons and ammunition. The trouble with the tigers has made the men extremely reluctant to go on scouting parties through the forest.

Considering everything, it isn't a bad planet; we could have had worse luck. We have tentatively named our new home, Earth II. After we had a small ceremony about the new name, I found some smart aleck had put up a sign, Earth Too.

Still can't get used to the three moons. The days are thirty hours long instead of twenty-four as earth's. The moons have such a rapid orbit that they seem to hurry across the sky at night just so they can be back during the day to cause weird eclipses as they pass between Earth II and our new sun.

I like the thirty hour days. On earth the days never seemed long enough. There were always so many things to be done and never enough time to do them. I used to sleep five hours a night. I still sleep five hours each night, and now the extra six hours waking time each day seems like a bonus that fate has finally given me.

2

Every muscle in Eric's body tensed. Although he instinctively reached for his knife, in the next instant he knew a knife would be useless.

But the dog was lifeless. Its skin was stained in a way he had never seen before and its head was misshapen. Sections of its hide were missing, and he could see part of a strange skelton within the creature's body.

"Bring it here."

Obediently, Eric reached into the compartment and withdrew the alien animal. After he had placed it next to the Tree Father's cushion, he knelt and stared in awe. There was so much to see! His eyes felt the way they had the morning when he awoke to find Alicia beside him naked.

"Your friend told you the truth," the old man said as he looked down at the dog. He indicated with a bony finger. "See this spot? And this? And this? That is the disease called rust. Touch it.''

Eric hesitated.

"Don't worry. It's not contagious. Humans don't rust.''

Gingerly, Eric touched the dog's disease. He pressed it between his fingertips and brought it close to his eyes. "It's like brown dust.''

"The rain, or water of any form, ruins the metal in the dog's body. Its joints especially. Some sections are more prone to the disease than others. It is, as you say, much like brown dust.''

Eric realized he was breathing deeply, excitedly. A metal dog! Here at his feet to examine! He had seen them a few times before, but only as they ran through the forest or fields. And then he had only glimpsed their skins shining in the sunlight.

"Is this the same—''

"No. This is not the dog your friend killed. One of our people brought me this one when it fell victim to the rust disease. I cracked its skull to see if its brains would break. Curiosity. Turn it over.''

Eric turned the creature on its other side. Part of the head had been removed and he could see the dog's brains. They were of wire and glass tubes. Most of the glass was broken and some of the wire had been torn by the blow on its head.

"Nothing magic,'' the older man said. "It has a metal head. The trick is to strike a blow hard enough to bend that metal down until it breaks the tubes.'' He laughed at the simplicity. Reaching to the shelves on the wall behind his cushion, he withdrew a slender object from its hiding place in a vase and held it before Eric's eyes. "Do you know what this is?"

"No." It resembled a knife, but the tip was rather blunt and squared.

"Screwdriver," the Tree Father said. "That's what it's called. We have no need of them, but the Techs use them to make their dogs and other things. They can be used to take a dog apart."

Following the instructions, Eric placed the screwdriver in one of the slots and tried to turn it but found it would not move.

"Turn the other way."

As he turned the screwdriver in the opposite direction, he watched in amazement as a piece of the metal dog rose until it fell away from the skin. He repeated the operation on all the slots he could find until he had loosened an entire section. Lifting the metal away and placing it aside, the metal dog's guts were exposed to his view. They were not at all like a tiger's guts. They were strange, hard objects, much like the wires and small odd tubes of the brains.

Holding the screwdriver in the palm of his hand, Eric studied it with admiration. "Then this could be a weapon as a club is a weapon against them."

The Tree Father shook his head sadly. "A screwdriver is good for taking a dog apart when it's dead, but it wouldn't be much of a weapon. Can you imagine trying to unscrew that thing while it gnawed at your throat? It would have your throat apart before you could get the first screw out!"

"The small pieces that hold it together are called screws?"

"Correct, my son. Did you know that the Guiders can see through the dogs' eyes?"

"I have heard such rumors but I cannot understand that kind of magic."

"There has been much evidence that the Guiders and Techs use the dogs as an extension of themselves and control their movements."

Eric was silent as he tried to digest those hard facts. He had seen the dogs running through the fields and forests. It was difficult to believe the Guiders and Techs could see what the dogs saw. Yet, if the Father said so, it must be the truth.

"There is another disease that befall the metal dogs," the Tree Father said. "A friend told me of it when I was very young. It is also caused by water and yet it is not like the rust disease that lingers. This other disease is quick, as quick as a man's heart can stop when he is old or sick. It is called short circuit. When it happens, it is called short-circuiting."

"Short-circuiting," Eric repeated carefully. This was another word he had not heard before. "What is this disease like, Father? Is it like the brown dust of rust, but of a different color?"

"It is not like any other metal dog disease. I do not understand it entirely, but I have been told it happens if an extreme amount of water strikes a dog, as in a heavy rain or if a dog should fall in a river. Then, I was told, the short-circuiting is like an internal fire. A metal dog's blood is a thing called electricity and too much water makes that blood flow so rapidly that it burns the veins."

"I see," Eric nodded solemnly at these words. He could only vaguely understand the concepts involved but there were still many things he did not comprehend.

"The Techs are lazy. They could make the dogs waterproof. They do not care. They make enough to serve the Guiders' purposes. Some are lost to rust and short-circuiting, but it is easier for the Techs to replace dead ones than build ones that would last much longer." The Tree Father glanced at a point on the wall near the ceiling. From a small, carved opening above the doorway, a shaft of sunlight extended across the room and fell upon symbols painted on the opposite wall. Everyone who could walk judged the time of day by the location of the sun in the sky. The Tree Father was crippled, could not walk to the windows to see the sun, and had devised his own unique timing device. The shaft of light was nearly invisible but its apex, a spot of sunlight moving slowly across the rows of symbols, was bright and clear. "It is almost noon. Ollie will be visiting shortly. Please replace that section of the dog. The screws will hold it together again. When putting it back, turn the screws in the opposite direction until they feel tight to your hand. We have spent enough time studying today. We must hide it again. Unlock and open the door."

Eric hurried to replace the section of the metal dog he had removed, hid it in its compartment, replaced the rug, unlocked and opened the door. He walked out onto the platform to glance down the length of the rope ladder that served as the Tree Father's main entrance. Each week the Father selected a different young boy to climb the rope to announce visitors. This week it was a small blond-haired boy. No one was ascending the rope, and although there was a group of boys playing near the ladder, he did not see any blond heads. The boy may be nearby, with a watchful eye on the ladder, but at least Ollie was not in sight yet. Good. He sat beside the Tree Father once more.

"Thank you for showing me the metal dog and explaining its diseases," Eric said respectfully.

"You are welcome," the Tree Father said gravely. Then, with a faint smile on his ancient lips, added, "As I told you when you were a boy and first came to me, I am more than a Father to tree people. A large tree must protect all who wish to come within cover of its branches. Hunters are always welcome."

So are Herb-Seekers and Butterfly-Catchers, Eric thought bitterly, but he had always felt that the Father held the greatest admiration for Hunters.

"I am glad you do not think my ambition is foolish," Eric said. That had been one of his greatest concerns.

"No," the Tree Father said slowly. "As I said before, many young men have come to me and confessed similar desires. It is a natural ambition and a small one compared to some." He paused. Eric saw that the ancient, gray eyes were focused directly on his face. "This should not be repeated. Some have come to me with dreams of revolting against the Guiders. They would like to reshape our society."

To Eric it seemed that the Tree Father was waiting for some reaction. He could not guess which response would please him most. The thought of revolution was shocking in its own peculiar way. It was like hearing someone say they would like to turn the nights into days, or change the flow of the Great

River from one direction to another. Yet, foolish as it may be, he secretly admired anyone who desired revolution. To want such a drastic change was a form of bravery in itself.

Alicia. Even now he was thinking of the touch of her soft lips against his lips, the fragrance of her hair, the curves of her body and the ecstasy that lay hidden within, like the sweetness deep within a purple nut. Glancing at the spot of sunlight on the Tree Father's timepiece across the room, he realized Alicia had become something like a disease within him. Not like the rust disease. More like the vines with bright yellow leaves, the vines that climbed some trees as far as the highest branches. It was difficult to distinguish vine from tree, as one engulfed the other. Memories of Alicia were constantly engulfing him. It was difficult to concentrate and think clearly at times because of the strength of the memories and his own desires they aroused. Now he sensed he had disappointed the Tree Father in some way. He could not comprehend the way. How? What had he said wrong?

A light rapid knock.

They looked up to see the blond-haired boy at the doorway. "Ollie is here, sir."

Eric had never liked the Herb-Seeker. He knew the Father favored him and, because of that, he had indulged in one of his few deceptions. For some time he had pretended to like the man and had often addressed him as one would address a friend.

"Send him up," Eric said to the boy. "I am finished and would like to speak to Ollie before I leave."

When they were alone again the Tree Father said, "Sometimes I feel like a physician with patients waiting in line." Before Eric could ponder how it must feel to be such an old man spending much time listening to problems and difficulties, the Father laughed and said, "But a physician loves his work and his patients. Without them he would be nothing."

"Greetings, Eric."

Ollie had appeared at the doorway and began to advance from the platform into the room. He was a short, thin man with large red-rimmed eyes. At times Eric had wondered if the redness in his eyes had been caused by eyestrain—the constant searching for herbs in fields, forests, and on mountainsides—or if the man had been born that way.

"Greetings, friend," Eric said, shaking the smaller man's hand and slapping him lightly on the back. (A hearty slap would have caused him to fall.)

"We must talk later," Ollie said eagerly. "You must tell me of your weekend and the woman. Do you have time for a game of chess?"

"Not today. We may have time to talk. I have to buy some rope but that should only take a few minutes."

"My visit with the Tree Father will be brief," Ollie said. "I have no great problems. I am conveying only some small news."

When Eric reached the bottom of the ladder, the blond-haired boy handed him his spear and the bag of items he had brought to trade with the Old Men. He had left the items in the visiting area reserved especially for such things. Climbing the seemingly endless rope to the house at the very top of the tree was work enough without carrying one's possessions.

"Thank you," said Eric.

The boy was looking at him with scarcely concealed admiration. A group of five or six boys stood nearby. They had ceased in the middle of some game, and Eric saw from the corner of an eye that they were watching him. Hunters were admired because they faced tigers and killed them. Eric could remember when he was a boy, he had admired Hunters as if they were fearless gods.

The blond-haired boy was staring at Eric's wide shoulders and strong arms and the many and sometimes deep scars that tigers had inflicted on them.

"They say you fear nothing," the boy whispered. He said it in such a way that it was as if he had thought aloud, rather than spoken something he had planned to say.

Eric felt a flush of embarrassment. He had never grown accustomed to admiration. He did not bask in it as some Hunters did. "What's your name?"

"Phillip."

He ruffled the boy's blond hair playfully. "Phillip, the point is not to fear nothing but to be prepared for anything. However, the best point of all is a sharp one." Laughing, Eric touched the tip of his spear with a finger. He was glad when the boy laughed, understanding and enjoying the analogy. He noticed that some boys had carved the outline of a tiger on the trunk of a large tree. A small inner circle represented the imaginary beast's heart. It was a game all young boys played no matter what they planned to be upon maturity. When a group played, the spear that struck the closest to the inner circle was the winning one. There were numerous variations of the game, sometimes with rewards for the winners, sometimes with punishments for the losers. As a boy, Eric had grown so adept with his spear that boys his own age had eventually refused to play the game with him. Afterwards he had practiced alone, endlessly, until one day he had gathered his nerve and joined a wandering group of Hunters. He was still so young that they had been reluctant to admit him to their group. After he demonstrated his skill with the spear, they had accepted him. At first his duties had been to sharpen the spears, skin the dead animals, and cook meals. But gradually they allowed him to participate in the hunts. Each animal that he speared had been a step from boyhood to Hunter until, before long, a younger boy joined their camp. The new one had then become the cook, and he, Eric, without formal declaration had become a Hunter.

It was a process that had evolved. It was not written anywhere, because only the Guiders and Techs knew how to write. Still, it was never mentioned or discussed in any way. If a boy wanted to be a Hunter, the desire in his blood was so strong that he sought their way of life. No one was ever invited to become a Hunter. With the passing years, Eric had realized that you do not invite someone to stand beside you and face death in the form of a hungry beast eager to devour your flesh. They are there because they want to be there, or they are not there at all.

24

As these things went quickly through his mind, he gave Phillip his spear. "Can you hit the tiger on the tree?"

Phillip accepted the spear, handling it carefully. It was much larger than his own spear, and the weight was unfamiliar. Eric watched with interest as the boy hefted the spear to gain the feel of its balance. Then, in one fluid movement, he hurled it at the tree. It struck the outline of the tiger, striking not near the heart but squarely on the flank.

It was a good shot, considering the fact that it was the first time the boy had handled the spear. "Good," Eric said, ruffling the blond hair again. "If that was a real tiger, he would die soon."

Retrieving his spear, Eric went to the group of old men who sat nearly a hundred feet away. Some of the older men had been watching Phillip and him, while others had remained engrossed in their work. It was a tradition among the Tree People that the older men became the craftsmen. This particular group were rope weavers and this was Eric's second motive for visiting the village today. He needed rope. At least three hundred feet of thin, lightweight, strong rope. After a few moments he saw the strength and thickness he wanted. He had brought a few items to trade. The old man who owned the rope did not seem especially concerned about its price, and Eric was thankful because some of the old ones would haggle over price for incredibly long periods of time.

As he finished concealing the rope in his bag, he noticed Ollie descending the ladder from the Tree Father's house.

"Let me buy you a drink," Ollie said cheerfully. They went to the winemaker a short distance away and the thin Herb-Seeker paid for two bottles, giving one to Eric. They sat with their backs against a tree and could see most of the village by turning to one side or the other: the ladder to the Tree Father's house, the groups of boys busy with their games, the old men engrossed in their work. All the underbrush in this area had been cleared away and the constant activity kept the ground hardened so that not even grass would grow. The trunks of the large trees stretched above them, their highest positions lost in the overlapping maze of branches and leaves. Most of the tree houses were hidden from view by leaves, but occasionally one could glimpse a portion of a house. The entrances to the dwellings varied. Some were rope ladders such as the one to the Father's house. These were most often used by the older men. Some of the ropes had been tied with thick knots at regular intervals. Others bore loops that allowed a climber to rest by inserting his feet in the loop to support his weight. And another kind was simply straight strands of rope. These were used by the youngest and strongest of the Tree People who could climb hand over hand with practiced skill. None of the ropes touched the ground. Most were at shoulder height and even the ladders for the old ones ended only knee-high above the ground.

Studying the various kinds of ropes, Eric made his decision. He had bought a thin and light, yet strong rope. Making a ladder from it would be absurd—it would then be too heavy to fling to the bridge that led to Alicia's tower. He would make one loop that would be three or four feet beneath the bridge. This would give him a resting place after he had captured Alicia and placed her on his shoulders. It might be necessary to adjust her weight. He could not yet decide if she would come willingly, under threat, or if he would have to knock her unconscious. In any event, the one loop would give him a place to settle the bulk of her body across his shoulders after he had started his descent from the bridge. If she was not conscious, then he would have to wrap her limp body around him, securing her in place by holding her wrists together. Perhaps it would be best to carry a small piece of rope to tie her hands together so both his hands could be free to maneuver the rope.

And then he decided that two knots spaced at equal distance would be a good safety measure. The rope would be thin and difficult to grasp. Besides that difficulty he would have the added weight. He did not expect to slip, but if he did, the knots would serve as stopping points to break his fall until he regained a proper grip.

Yes. One loop and two knots.

"You are very quiet today," Ollie said. He had been quiet enough himself, busy emptying the contents of the bottle.

"Thinking," Eric replied noncommittally.

"About the woman."

Eric nodded that this was true, although he was certain Ollie would be startled if he could read his mind and see how he planned to steal the woman.

"I have been saving my herbs," Ollie said. "Soon I will have enough to pay the Guiders for a weekend with a woman." His smile was a sly and happy one. Eric fought a vague inner resentment. Ollie, a Herb-Seeker, could enjoy the pleasures of a woman simply by searching the fields and forest for the rare herbs that the Guiders valued so much. The work did not require bravery or even a decent amount of physical effort.

"What was her name?" Ollie asked.

"Alicia."

"Ah. A pretty name. Will you tell me about her?"

He had known Ollie a long time. Because the Tree Father favored him for some unfathomable reason, he had pretended friendship with the weak man in order to further cement his relationship with the Father. In some measure the pretended amity had become partially a real one. This, and the fact that the wine had begun to loosen his tongue, caused him to speak of Alicia. He said many things that he would not have told anyone else. He told how beautiful she was. He went into much detail of the joys he had experienced with her.

"Ah," Ollie said. "When I have gathered enough herbs, I think I will ask the Guiders for a weekend with *her*."

Eric reacted instinctively and unthinkingly as he would have before a charging tiger. His muscles were suddenly independent of his mind. He rose, grasping Ollie by the throat and hauling him erect. His fist smashed the small man's chin with such an impact that Ollie toppled backward, struck the tree, and bounced forward to fall face down on the hard ground.

The thin man rolled on his back and shifted slowly to a sitting position. His lip was split and there was a great deal of blood on his mouth and chin. His slender fingers dabbled at the stickiness of blood in a dazed manner as if he had been struck by an unexpected bolt of fire from the sky.

Eric straightened his fingers, staring at his own fist as it slowly unfolded. He, too, was dazed by his unexpected reaction.

Others had noticed. The boys, the old men . . . A silence fell through the forest, and Eric could see they were all looking at Ollie and him, their wide eyes filled with the question:

Why?

A Hunter was strong and quick. A Hunter had to be strong. Herb-Seekers and Butterfly-Catchers were the weaklings of the race, yet they were shown respect because they worked. For a Hunter to strike a Herb-Seeker was a violation of ethics. It was almost as foul as striking a defenseless boy.

And, now, all the silent eyes were asking why.

Besides that unspoken question, Eric could see something else in the many eyes. Respect and admiration had vanished. The seeds of distrust and hatred had been planted. Ollie was well-liked by all the Tree People. Although he spent many hours searching for the rare herbs, he had often unselfishly given them to the sick and the poor whenever needed, often without ever being repaid.

Eric picked up his spear and his bag.

He could not say he was sorry, he could not explain, because he did not fully understand. The world had changed suddenly. It had become a

29

meaningless place, and only two things made even the slightest sense: his spear was a weapon to kill tigers, and the bag contained the rope he needed to reach Alicia's tower.

As he left the village of the Tree People, he could feel their eyes on his back. The silence remained like a heavy weight. Long after he was beyond sight of the village, he felt as if their eyes and silence still rested on his shoulders.

Entry in Captain Farrell's personal diary, March, 2376:

I lost track of the days. It is some time in March by earth time. Who cares? I guess we'll have to make our own calendars.

No. Our navigator calculated it takes Earth Two about 1500 days to make a complete orbit of this sun. That means a yearly calendar would be four times the length of an earth calendar. Too complicated, and the psychological effect might be bad, causing something similar to the temporal disassociation felt by so many who tried the suspended animation trips.

I feel weary. Our farm projects are not going well enough to sustain the colony. We still need to send hunters to kill any kind of animal they can find— anything edible, and the tigers are taking their toll. We are running low on ammunition and have begun manufacturing spears. I thought I was tough. I am not so tough. I find I love these men as if they were my own sons. When one dies, I feel as if I have lost a son.

Did ancient generals such as Napoleon and Pat-

ton feel the same? They must have felt differently, more impersonal. They had so many men under their command.

The rate of our losses has declined and it seems we are adjusting to the alien metabolism, but we lost many more than I expected.

A hundred graves.

Two hundred of us left to fight this damned planet.

3

After Alicia bathed and dressed and combed her hair, she went to stand by the window where she had last seen Eric. It had been a wonderful weekend, *he* had been wonderful. At first the scars on his body had frightened her, but then she had grown accustomed to seeing them. It was the first time she had ever been with a Hunter. She had not realized that a man could be so satisfying in so many ways. On their last morning, after they kissed and said farewell, she had stood by this window and watched him cross the fields to the edge of the forest. He had stopped at the edge and paused, turning to look back. She had waved, but the distance had been too great and he had not seen her. At such a distance he must have been able to see her tower clearly enough, but the window must have appeared as a tiny dark slit.

The bridge alarm buzzed to notify her that someone was on the way to her tower. With a tinge of annoyance, she pressed the button to silence the noise. The Guiders were so protective that often they were a pain in the neck. All the towers were interconnected by bridges, but they were so far above the ground that neither man nor beast could reach them. Why have such a stupid precaution?

Someone knocked on her door. She knew by the sound that it was her friend Maria. Without hesitating she unlocked and opened the door.

"Good morning, Maria."

"Good morning, Alicia."

Maria was a short, plump, dark-haired girl with a continuous smile and ingratiating manner. She thrived on friendships and affection, and therefore sought and maintained friends as if they were food for her soul. Alicia was one of her closest friends.

"How was he?" Maria asked. "Was he very good?"

It embarrassed Alicia to discuss men as if they were animals or objects of pleasure, but to maintain the friendship with Maria she had always successfully stifled this minor friction. "He was strong."

"Very strong?" Maria asked eagerly. Her eyes were twinkling.

"Yes." Maria had dropped to a cluster of cushions in one corner and Alicia went to sit beside her. She had entertained only a few men before Eric. She had not minded discussing them, but now for a reason she could not quite understand she did not really want to discuss Eric and the things they had done. It was as if the time they spent together had become something precious that should be kept private and protected.

"He was a big man, wasn't he?" Maria asked. "I saw him as the Guiders brought him here." She frowned. "I could tell he was a Hunter. I wonder why is it that you and some of the others always seem to get big strong Hunters while I and Helen always get Herb-Seekers and Butterfly-Catchers?" She frowned thoughtfully.

Alicia gave the mystery some consideration. Maria and Helen were short and dark-haired and plump. There must be something about short, dark, plump women that appealed to Herb-Seekers and Butterfly-Catchers. The Hunters seemed to favor tall, slender, blonde women. Although she had noticed the evidence of the preferences, she could not understand the reasons behind them.

"Do you think he will come again next weekend to see you?" Maria asked.

"I hope so." And purely for effect because she knew it was expected of her, she giggled girlishly.

While they were sitting and talking, the dark thoughts crept into her mind. It was strange, something new, because she was sitting comfortably in her tower with all her beautiful possessions—the flowers and paintings and precious books, colorful cushions and draperies—yet two words rang in her mind:

Next weekend?

She hoped he would come again, but would there ever be another weekend with Eric? The scars on his body were testimony to the fact that he had come close to death many times. The Herb-Seekers and Butterfly-Catchers and Tree People did not face such dangers. Eric could die violently, unexpectedly. Any day, any moment. That would be the end. She would never see him again. It was such a simple, uncomplicated realization, but it made her suddenly afraid. Despite Maria's presence, she felt lonely.

Eric filled the days with work. First he had to find a rarely visited section of the Valley of the Tigers and, secondly, a tree branch approximately the height of a tower bridge. When he found the right branch, he spent one whole day carving a portion of the wood until it was rectangular, as close to the dimensions of the bridge railings that his eye could recall.

He had visualized the type of hook needed. Fashioning it was much more difficult than inventing it in his mind. One hook proved insufficient. It twisted and would not hold properly. Two hooks were better, but there was a certain difficulty in the swinging and throwing. In the end he found that three hooks worked perfectly. With practice, he could swing, throw, and catch the high branch nine times out of ten. He ascended and descended a few times to gain skill with the rope.

Feeling foolish, he made a dummy the approximate size of a woman and filled it with a mixture of dirt and straw until the weight was as close as he could estimate. During this practice session, he had been hoping that no one would see him. When he reached the point of practicing with the dummy, he began to *pray* that no one would observe his

35

seemingly idiotic behavior.

He practiced with the dummy for two whole days. Since the dummy did not have a life of its own, he had to tie its wrists together and more or less hang its weight over his shoulders. Alicia might hang onto him willingly. She might want to come to the forest with him. But the only logical course was to assume that she would resist and that he would have to carry her unconscious body after he knocked her out.

There were a few mishaps and he learned some things. Although the first descent went well, the second did not. The dummy's wrists slid and lodged against his throat, the weight nearly strangling him before he could reach the ground. When he tried to forestall that eventuality by holding his chin close to his chest when he had the dummy on his back, the circle of bound wrists skidded up his nose and over his forehead, the dummy falling to the ground shortly after he began the descent. He had stared at the spread-eagled dummy far below with wide-eyed dismay. If that had been the real Alicia the fall would have broken every bone in her body.

After giving the matter some thought, he found a method of placing one of the dummy's arms over a shoulder, with the other arm under his own arm on the opposite side. That method, with the dummy's wrists securely bound, allowed him to descend rapidly with no risk of dropping the precious cargo. He practiced until carrying the weight down the rope seemed nearly as natural as walking.

Satisfied with his methods and equipment, he had only to wait until the right night. He wanted a cloud-filled one. Sometimes the clouds were so thick they hid all the light from the stars and three moons. Such darkness would hide him from any woman who happened to look out her tower window.

It would be too much to hope for a rain-filled night, a storm. Such would be ideal. It would give darkness, and the women would close the shutters on their tower windows. Furthermore, the metal dogs could not follow him for at least a day or a day and a half after the rain. It had been observed over the years that the dogs never traveled forth until such a length of time had passed after a rainfall. The various tribes had attributed this fact to some sort of strange superstition on the metal dogs' part. Now, after the talk with the Tree Father, Eric knew it was because of the rust and short-circuited diseases. The forests were filled with sections where the bushes were thick and did not dry completely until a day or more following a rain.

The bridge to Alicia's tower would sound an alarm when he walked on it. He had seen this happen during the weekend with Alicia. One of her women friends had visited and knocked on the door for it to be opened. On the night that he went to steal Alicia, she would hear the alarm. He would have to knock as if he were a visiting friend. He hoped Alicia would quickly open the door without asking who knocked. If she did, all should go well because he was quite expert at throwing the rope with its hook and descending it with a woman's approximate size and weight. It would be Alicia's choice. Come with him willingly and hang onto him. Otherwise he would tie her wrists and take her forcefully.

He killed four more tigers during the following days. Now, ironically, he had enough payment to spend another weekend with Alicia. But why? Why torture himself with another taste of the cake when he had a good plan to steal the whole thing?

While waiting for the right night, he bought some bottles of wine. Impatient, frustrated and tortured by his own plans, he drank heavily. Every night was a bright moonlit night. The sky did not show promise of clouds or rain.

One afternoon he found himself stumbling into the Tree People's village. Ollie was sitting at the base of the tree that held his hut. Eric, as if awakening from a dream, realized he had been carrying the ten tiger skins and two bottles. Ollie leaped to his feet upon sight of the Hunter. Their last encounter had been extremely painful.

"For you," he said thickly. "To buy a woman for a weekend."

Ollie's eyes bulged unbelievingly. Villagers had noticed Eric's arrival. Some of the younger men had come forth in a tentative manner, standing at a distance some yards behind Eric. If he struck Ollie again, the young men had decided, it would be a long long time before Eric ever struck anyone else. They had also planned to reshape his face somewhat, with a removal of some teeth. Ollie, thin and weak, had befriended many by his generous gifts of medicinal herbs when someone was ill. He had been especially kind toward the old men who were often unable to repay. It had been decided that since Ollie lacked the physical strength to protect

38

himself, *they* would protect him.

But upon seeing Eric drop the ten tiger skins at Ollie's feet, the young men hesitated. There were more than a dozen men gathering in a semicircle behind Eric, and they were all about Eric's and Ollie's age. The gift of ten tiger skins was a staggering, priceless gift. No man had ever given so many, even as a gift of friendship.

Eric held the two bottles of wine toward Ollie. "Which you want?"

"They both look the same."

"Which?"

"It doesn't make any difference."

"Pick one."

Ollie chose one and held it in a hand that shook slightly. He was not frightened. He was more surprised than he had ever been before. He watched as Eric drew the cork from his own bottle. "You drink that one," Eric said. "I'll drink this one." He frowned as if it had taken a great deal of effort to calculate the mathematics.

The young men began to disperse. It was obvious that Ollie would not need protection, evident that Eric had come in friendship. Seeing his condition, some marveled as to how he had been able to reach the village. They doubted he would be able to leave under his own will later in the evening.

Sitting side by side with their backs against the tree trunk, Eric and Ollie consumed the contents of the bottles. Ollie bought two more.

After they had been sitting for a long time in silence, Eric felt the need to start a conversation.

"The Tree Father has a fondness for purple

nuts,'' he said solemnly.

"I know,'' Ollie agreed. "He mentioned it to me also.''

"We must bring him a sack of purple nuts some day.''

Ollie nodded his head in agreement, and that was the end of the conversation. At one point they tried a chess game but it did not work out too well; their hands had a tendency to knock the pieces down rather than pick them up. Eric sometimes saw two of every chess piece, sometimes three. It made playing so difficult that he said, "I concede.'' Ollie, leaning over the board and peering at it myopically, protested mildly, "You were winning,'' but nevertheless took the board and chess pieces and put them aside. He ascended the ladder to his tree hut and returned a considerable time later with a bag of herbs which he placed at Eric's feet.

"Enough to buy a woman for a weekend,'' Ollie said.

"Thank you.''

Eric was glad his friendship with Ollie had been repaired. He could not bring himself to tell the other man that he was sorry he had hit him. He was still not quite sure of his reason. He had now consumed so much wine that it was difficult to reason anything.

"I know why you hit me,'' Ollie said abruptly, as if reading Eric's muddled thoughts.

"Why did I?''

"Jealousy.''

"Mmmm.'' Eric considered this diagnosis for awhile with pursed lips, frowning thoughtfully, and then nodded his head in agreement. Afterwards they were both sad and silent for awhile as they continued to drink. To admit to having succumbed to jealousy was nearly as bad as contracting the Black Plague or the Caucasian Rot. It was not as fatal but being jealous of another's interest in a woman was, in a sense, socially embarrassing. The Guiders had trained them that women were pleasurable objects to be worked for and to be used. To become emotionally involved enough to be jealous was a sign of an emotional disturbance so complex that it drew great pity from others. No one understood the disease called jealousy—its roots and food, at least. The end results and effects were often plain enough. Dwelling upon the subject now, Eric reflected that man's disease of jealousy was much like the metal dog's disease of rust. Both could be seen but not understood.

Why should water cause a metal dog to rust? Why should he be jealous if Ollie was interested in Alicia or spent a weekend with her?

The wise Guiders had declared The System. It had been in use for hundreds of years since their rebirth from the planet Earth. The System had been proven. It worked. Jealousy was like a rebellion against the Guiders and their laws.

He was aware of dealing with one of the old men for a sack of purple nuts. He had explained they were for the Tree Father, and, that being so, the old man said, he could have the sack for half price. Ollie was standing nearby, still drinking from one of the wine bottles and swaying precariously. Several of the old men sitting on the ground in the group kept a wary eye on Ollie, lest they have to cushion his fall.

The transaction had been completed. Eric had slipped the sack in his pocket and grinned. Tomorrow he and Ollie could take the purple nuts to the Tree Father.

A Tech stumbled through the edge of forest and into the clearing. The entire village of Tree People were motionless as if suddenly and magically paralyzed. The sun was setting below the horizon. It was that time of day when you could watch the darkness of night creep through the forest steadily and silently.

He was a young Tech. Very young. He smiled at everyone.

Techs were not permitted in the village, or in the forest, except when on Survey Teams of three. The System said that Techs were to stay at Homebase and tend to their particular duties.

"Freedom," the Tech said. *"Freedom!"* He tilted his head back and drew a deep breath of air, expanding his chest. "Fresh air. It tastes great."

The Tech was carrying a strange metallic object in one hand. Eric tried to focus his eyes on it. With great difficulty he managed to reduce the blurriness of the object, but even so he could still not identify it.

Five metal dogs moved silently from the forest. The Tech extended his arm and pointed the object at one. A beam of light struck the dog and it fell to one side, lifeless. The Tech aimed the object at another dog, but this time there was no beam of light. The young man stared at the object in his hand, shook it, and . . .

The four remaining metal dogs had formed a circle around the Tech. Eric knew they were closing in for the kill and instinctively started toward his spear.

But the old man who sold him the purple nuts was suddenly erect, grasping his arm, whispering, "No. You can't stop it."

One of the dogs leaped toward the Tech's throat.

Entry in Captain Farrell's diary, 2376:

There are times when the origin of a particular status quo seems to fade away and become lost in the obscurity of the past. And the problems of the present tend to make the exact causes seem less and less important. We are here, a voice whispers. The past cannot be changed. We must deal with the present to form the future.

So, it seems incredible now to think that we were once a part of a huge intergalactic army. If the Corsair had arrived at its original destination, the three nurses on our ship would have been guarded as they were transported to a hospital with hundreds of other nurses. The soldiers would have been soon transferred to another planet where we were fighting hand-to-hand. Ironically, both we and the aliens had so far avoided the use of nuclear weapons because the combat was so integrated that to use them would mean killing as many of one's own army as of the enemy. Such details are relatively unimportant now. I do wonder, however, if the aliens defeated mankind. Perhaps, we, the sur-

vivors of the Corsair's accident in space, are the last of mankind. If so, we have a duty to our race to survive.

During the last week there were no volunteers to search the forests for food. Too many casualties to the tigers. I had to order a roster prepared. I have to order the men into the forest each day and always there are some who do not return. The men have begun to hate me. They do not seem to comprehend we will all die of malnutrition if we do not constantly replenish our food supply.

A thought occurred. A possible solution. Some of the men (most) are so starved for female companionship that they would give their right arm to only talk with one of the nurses.

If I had not earned my captain's rank as a chaplain, if I were a captain in any other branch of the Army, the men would probably have killed me weeks ago when I placed the nurses in carefully guarded quarters.

But why not establish some sort of reward system? The man who returns with the most food—or the most tiger skins (as proof of his conquest)—will be awarded a certain number of hours with the nurse of his choice.

It should work much better than any impartial alphabetical system. A man approached me yesterday and pleaded, "Sir, can I talk with one of the nurses for a few minutes? I haven't talked to a woman in months!"

That seems to be the general feeling of the men. The incentive might work very well.

4

Eric did not feel good when he awakened. His head throbbed so badly that for a moment he thought someone had split his skull with an axe and that somehow he had not died. His stomach did not feel too bad. It felt as if there were some butterflies in there—maybe a thousand or so—fluttering around frantically as they tried to get out. It was a mild sensation compared to the one in his head.

He'd fallen asleep among the group of old men. During the summer months they often slept on the ground rather than climbing into the tree huts each night. One of them was peering at him now. Seeing that Eric's eyes were open, he said, "Here. Drink this."

Eric drank the cup of liquid. He could not remember its name but he remembered it was a cure for the bad physical sensations after drinking too much. He rarely drank at all, but he had during the past years drunk to excess two or three times, so the unpleasant sensations were not new to him.

"Thank you."

He settled down on the ground again, closing his eyes. He drifted between sleep and consciousness.

The memories of the night before came to him. The Tech, the dogs. He grimaced when he remembered how the metal dogs had ripped the Tech's throat apart. The dogs were as vicious as any tiger. With a difference. A tiger killed for food, or to rid himself of an enemy, or to leave a small dead bait in the hope of luring bigger game. Basically a tiger killed to live. But the metal dogs were not alive and were controlled by Techs within Homebase. When one of the dogs killed, it was because of some offense against the Guiders or The System.

Still half asleep, Eric frowned. The Guiders had so many rules and regulations and laws. A Tech was subordinate to a Guider. Eric did not understand the exact gap but he had heard enough about the many rules and regulations and laws to know it must be damned hard not to displease a Guider. It must be one of the main worries in a Tech's life.

Luckily the Guiders did not concern themselves with Hunters, Tree People, Herb-Seekers and Butterfly-Catchers. It had been obvious by their behavior that they simply didn't care what the people in the forest did—except when they visited Homebase to trade items for a weekend with a woman. Then they were subject to all the rules and regulations.

But what had the Tech done?

He had come into the forest alone.

The Guiders had a rule that Techs had to travel at

least in threes when moving through the forest.

Why? Why was a group of three so important?

Important enough to kill a man?

The Tech had used some thing that had killed one of the dogs.

He opened his eyes. One of the Old Men was looking in another direction. After a few minutes he turned slowly and glanced casually down at Eric, noticing his eyes were open again.

Eric said, "What happened to that thing the Tech used to kill one of the dogs?" A slim hope had begun to stir. Whatever it was, if it was still here in the village, maybe he could examine it and determine how it worked. It would be most useful.

"One of the dogs took it in his mouth and carried it away," the old man explained.

"Too bad."

"Why?"

Eric had to be careful about what he said. He had told no one except the Tree Father about his plans to steal Alicia. He joked, "Since it killed a dog, I wanted to see if it would kill a tiger."

The old man grunted. "It only killed one dog. Then it did not work again. A spear that breaks with each throw would be no good."

"Is the metal dog still here?"

"No. The other two dogs dragged it away. We thought they would leave the Tech's body, but four more dogs came and dragged the body into the forest."

"All the way to Homebase?"

The old man shrugged. "Who knows? No one wanted to follow to see. I think some were afraid and some wanted to sleep. The others did not care."

Eric closed his eyes and drifted soundly asleep. It was nearly noon when he awakened again. He visited the Tree Father and gave him the sack of purple nuts. In return, the Father forced him to eat something for lunch.

Ollie visited also and the three talked awhile.

The throbbing in Eric's head ceased. The butterflies in his stomach went away. He slept a few more hours while Ollie and the Tree Father talked.

When he awakened, he rose and stretched, yawning. With his arms still extended in a V above his head, he froze. Dark clouds were scudding across the horizon. Nearer and nearer.

It would rain tonight.

The sky would be dark from the clouds and, if still not raining, it would surely have rained sometime during the late afternoon or evening. The rain would retard the progress of the metal dogs when they pursued him.

His heartbeat quickened with excitement. He would steal Alicia tonight.

When he turned to look in the Tree Father's direction, he saw the old man had been studying him thoughtfully. He finished chewing one of the purple nuts and then said emotionlessly, "Tonight is the night, isn't it?"

"Yes."

"I could see it in your eyes."

"It will rain soon. The rain will help drown our trail either tonight or tomorrow."

"And you are anxious to have your woman again, aren't you?"

48

Eric found himself blushing. The Tree Father was teasing. Eric responded, "Yes."

"I have a gift for you." The Tree Father opened a wooden box and withdrew a knife. "Bring the metal dog here and I will show how this knife is much different than other knives."

Eric removed the metal dog from the hidden compartment under the round rug and brought it across the room to place beside the Tree Father.

The older man said, "No ordinary knife can penetrate metal."

The knife resembled other knives, but Eric could see the metal of the blade was a different color than usual and the handle bore a large ruby. The Tree Father held the ruby knife above the flank of the metal dog and said, "This knife will help if you have to kill one of the dogs at close range. See? When you press the blade against metal, it is like any other knife. But press the ruby and . . ."

The Tree Father continued to hold the knife against the metal surface as he pressed the ruby with his thumb. Eric heard a faint humming sound. The knife appeared to vibrate in the Father's hand, and the metal parted beneath the shimmering blade. Eric stared in amazement as the blade sank deep into the mechanical animal. The Tree Father brought the knife out in a slashing motion that continued to rend the metal.

"Magic," Eric heard himself whisper in awe.

"Of a sort," the Tree Father replied softly. "Not precisely magic. However, it is a form of science we are not familiar with."

"How does it work?"

"I have heard it described as a type of molecular vibration. But I am afraid neither of us has the scientific education to understand exactly how it functions." The Father had released his thumb from the ruby and the strange vibrating stopped. He held the knife by the blade and extended it toward Eric. "I would advise you to keep it with you always. And tell no one that it is different than an ordinary knife. I know of only one other knife such as this one."

Eric accepted the gift, removing his old knife and laying it on the floor, sliding the jeweled knife into the sheath on his belt. He felt a strong surge of emotion at this gesture on the Tree Father's part and struggled to keep it from showing on his face or in his voice.

Trying to focus his mind in other directions, he said, "Who owns the other knife?"

"I will tell you someday," the Tree Father said. "Return with your Alicia. I would like to meet her, and perhaps I will tell you then."

Eric nodded that he would return some day for the answer. "I have to go now, Father," he said quietly. "I have to gather tools I have prepared, and it will take some time to reach Alicia's tower."

"Come here," the Tree Father said, extending his arms.

Eric moved closer and the older man embraced him. He felt deeply moved as the frail hands patted his back. "I have never said this before, but I have always thought of you as my true son. My son, Eric. If I had fathered a son, I would want him to be like you. Promise to keep the knife with you always."

"I promise."

50

"It will bring you luck."

As Eric moved away, he glimpsed the Tree Father's eyes and saw they were moist. He felt flooded with a mixture of emotions as he left. Instinctively, he sensed the dangers that lay ahead. They were varied and numerous, and any of the many dangers could mean death if he made a mistake.

He felt strangely satisfied in a way. He had lived in a society where few men knew the identity of their father or mother. It was something that all men on this world had learned to live with in one way or another, although quite often commonplaceness had not lessened the hunger for an exact identity. Eric had frequently felt the desire to know his father. Now the Tree Father's declaration had dissolved the emptiness and the hunger, he felt as if he now had a true father.

And mingled with the tense awareness of danger and the satisfaction of a lifelong hunger, he felt a great and new type of anticipation that seemed to grow stronger with every passing moment. This was the night he would steal Alicia.

Entry in Captain Farrell's diary, 2376:

I never thought I would see the day when the men would mutiny.

It was very quiet and orderly. They were as gentle as possible but still using force. I am confined to a cell.

They secretly decided upon a new type of government. They call it 'democratic.' They will have a ruling body called 'Guiders' and they say many of my programs will be continued.

I do not agree with much of their reasoning. They say this world is too barbaric and unfriendly for a chaplain to have complete authority.

If Major Coulson and Colonel Webb had not died shortly after our arrival, the responsibility would not have been placed in my hands at all. I was the highest ranking officer.

Now the men will shape the colony and its future by their own decisions, supposedly by the wishes of the majority and the wisdom of the 'Guiders.'

While helpless physically, I will pray they use their new power wisely.

5

He was both pleased and surprised as the grappling hook caught the railing on the first try. Even when he last practiced with the tree branch, he had not always been able to throw the hook perfectly enough to catch the first time during each practice session.

The rain had stopped a few minutes before, but the sky was still filled with dark clouds and he was nearly invisible in the night as he ascended the rope.

Over the railing and onto the bridge.

He knew the alarm would ring in Alicia's tower. During the weekend that he spent with her, she had never seemed startled or disturbed when hearing the alarm. It was more than anything else, at least to her, merely a way of giving advance warning that a guest was arriving. He knocked on the door, imitating a woman's light knock.

Several minutes passed. He knocked again.

Was something wrong? Had Alicia gone to one of the other towers to visit a friend? Was she asleep, so soundly asleep that she could not hear his knock? Several possibilities burst in his mind along with nameless fears. Everything could go wrong. His whole plan could turn into a disaster.

The door opened.

He was paralyzed for a moment and he felt a lump in his throat. She was so beautiful, standing there in the doorway, framed by the light from behind, her long hair floating around her shoulders, the silhouette of her slender body one sensuous curve blending into another.

He pushed past her, closed the door.

"Will you hang onto me or will I have to tie your wrists?" he blurted.

Her eyes widened with alarm. She was trembling. Her lips moved soundlessly awhile and then formed the word, *"What?"*

"Will you—" Eric caught himself, blushed when he realized how idiotic the question had sounded. He had been so engrossed in the unanswerable element of whether Alicia would come willingly or not, that he had not even explained his intentions! "I want you to come with me," he said hastily. "I have a rope up to the bridge. I have to take you down the rope. You can hold onto my back as I climb down, or I'll tie your wrists together and carry you."

Alicia sank into a pillow and shuddered. This was the most startling thing that had ever happened to her in her whole life, this muscular brute of a man appearing at her tower in the middle of the night, saying all these strange things.

"You want me to go with you?" she repeated unbelievingly.

"Yes."

"But *where?*"

"A place in the Valley of the Tigers."

She closed her eyes and ran a hand across her forehead. She said, "But *why?*"

"Then we will be together. Always. No one will ever separate us." His voice had risen in volume. He spoke with defiance now—not at her, but at the society they lived within, the frustrating maze of customs and laws that had and would keep them apart for long periods of time.

"Together," she repeated numbly. She looked up at him, understanding brightening her face and widening her eyes once more.

"As in the old days," Eric said. "Before man came to Earth Two. We will be husband and wife."

She could not look away from the gray of his eyes. They were magnetic, transfixing her gaze. The full meaning of what he was saying struck her with the impact of a bolt of lightning. Husband and wife. It was something that she and the other women had talked about from time to time and it had been like the other fantastic unreachable things in that faraway place called Earth. Marriage was another word for it. But it had always seemed like a fairy tale. Like the stories about metal birds called jets that carried people thousands of feet in the air at tremendous speeds, of huge stores where a person could buy anything she desired, or subways that carried people underground.

"Which will it be?" Eric asked.

"They—they'll send the metal dogs after us."

"I know of ways to kill metal dogs. They will not harm you. I promise."

She rose, biting her lower lip in indecision. She felt helpless and confused. Husband and wife. Marriage. This was something she had never seriously considered as a possibility—the way she knew she would never fly in a jet, or shop at a huge store that sold everything, or ride in a subway. The concept was staggering. To be with a man for your whole life, every day?

There were many hours in the tower when she ached with loneliness. During these past days she had thought of Eric almost constantly.

During her indecision, he came to her and placed his arms around her. Gently, very gently, he lowered his head and pressed his lips against hers in the kissing motion she had taught him. She clung to him, her heart beating more rapidly as memories swelled within her.

When the kiss ended at last, she said weakly, "I'll go with you."

"Good." He smiled and she felt as if, by her agreement, she had completed a new union. It was not physical. It was of the mind and of those invisible things the Guiders called heart and soul. With a growing excitement, she realized this was a permanent union between Eric and herself. Nothing could break it. Perhaps even death would not end it.

Guider Thomas burst into the control room. He was breathing deeply because he had been running.

As he closed the door, he struggled to slow his heart-beat. He did not want to appear overly excited. He said, "Alicia is gone."

"Gone? What do you mean by gone?" Bromfield leaped to his feet. He had been elected Guider President because of many reasons. He was strong and intelligent and cold and calculating. Before his election, the other Guiders had judged him to be a fair man. Some still thought he judged fairly, but more and more of the Guiders had begun to suspect that President Bromfield contained a concealed streak of ruthlessness.

"She's left her tower," Thomas said.

"How?"

"With a man."

"Who saw this happen?"

"Her friend Maria. She went to visit Alicia. She was at the far end of the bridge."

"Did she recognize the man?"

"No. She couldn't see his face and she's sure they didn't see her."

Bromfield rubbed his chin thoughtfully. "Eric. The Hunter Eric. He spent last weekend with her. Ten tiger skins." He shook his head and laughed. The sound was like a bark. "Any man who isn't afraid of tigers, isn't afraid of *anything*." His dark eyes swung suddenly to focus on Thomas. "Was Alicia conscious?"

"Maria said she was walking and the man didn't seem to be forcing her to go. But I was thinking that doesn't necessarily mean she went willingly. He may have threatened her. He might have said he'd kill her if she didn't go with him."

President Bromfield nodded and turned to Guider Wesley who sat at the console. He had been sitting there absolutely motionless and silent during the conversation. He was a pale, slender man with wispy hair and large eyes. "Wesley, put X-20 on the run."

Wesley hesitated. "It's still in the experimental stage. We don't know—"

"This will be a damned good time to find out what it will do and what it won't," Bromfield said. "And put twelve of the regulars on the trail, five minutes behind X-20."

Alicia felt completely exhausted. They had been moving through the forest for hours. Although she could not see the sun for the maze of trees that blocked her view, she had seen the deep shadows gradually gray and disappear. It was morning. Eric rarely looked at her, nothing more than an occasional backward glance as if to make sure she was still there, following in his path. He seemed to have an inexhaustible amount of strength, and he was not even breathing hard after all the hours of walking, though she felt as if she might collapse any moment.

They climbed a hill. Eric took her hand to help her up the incline.

At the edge of the cliff, he had a fleeting glimpse of the metal dogs far behind them, moving slowly in a single file across a clearing. They wouldn't have much time.

"Can you swim?" he asked as he looked down at

the river.

"Yes." She had collapsed on the ground. She was trembling with both fear and fatigue.

"We won't have long to rest. Only a few minutes. Then all we have to do is to jump into the river and swim to the other side. The dogs won't be able to follow us. They'll have to go miles upstream before they reach narrow places where they can cross on fallen trees. By that time we'll be in the Valley of the Tigers and they'll never find us."

Alicia made a strange sound in her throat. It was not a scream, it was a moan of terror that chilled Eric's blood. She was looking at something in the bushes beyond him, and when he turned, he saw the dog.

It had been standing there, waiting for him, watching them as they talked. It had come before the other dogs now crossing the field in the valley below. It was different than all the other metal dogs he had seen in the past. It was larger and its skin did not gleam—its skin was like a dull brown fur . . .

The dog leaped, its sharp teeth glinting in the morning sunlight as they flashed for Eric's throat. The weight slammed against him, and he felt himself falling as he simultaneously felt the pain of the dog's teeth. He had known fear before but never defeat. Now he felt a bitter taste of defeat as he fell, his ears ringing with Alicia's screams.

Entry in Captain Farrell's diary:

First I lost track of the days, then the months, and now, finally, I do not know what year it is by earth time.

Not that it matters.

The Guiders seem to be governing well.

During the past years, the nurses have had twenty-five children. The disturbing factor is that only five were female and twenty were male.

This ratio is not in accordance with birth statistics on earth. No one in the colony is experienced in genealogy, but some of the Guiders have theorized that the ratio is due to a planetary influence which, they admit, they do not understand fully. A study of all other living creatures on this planet had indicated approximately the same ratio of birth rate, male to female.

One of the Guiders has discovered that, for instance, there are approximately ten male tigers for each female. The general understanding is that this is such a harsh world that male strength is needed in a predominant quantity for the survival of any given species. This was far from the case on earth. Even the Canada geese mated one-to-one for life!

The established walled-in colony has been named Homebase, and already there are tentative plans to send young males into the forests when they reach puberty. I do not like this plan, no matter how strongly the Guiders feel it would be following the necessary survival pattern. To keep Homebase from becoming overpopulated, they would adopt a survival of the fittest program. It would be as barbaric as this world.

Yet, the Guiders say it may be necessary.

If this plan is carried out, I feel our colony will develop into a type of society mankind has never seen before. It will not necessarily be immoral, but the classes will be ironclad. I think democracy will be a word rather than a fact, the weak will die, and the strong will survive.

Tremendous power and authority may easily fall into the wrong hands.

6

Eric's shoulders crashed against the water. He had raised his arm in defense and the dog had sunk its sharp teeth into his flesh. He knew his attacker's next move would be to swing its head from side to side and ruthlessly rip his arm apart. They were sinking beneath the surface, and the dog seemed frozen by surprise at their strange, watery surroundings. Eric knew that if the fight had progressed on the ground he would have been mortally wounded by this time. The river had given him a few moments to make another move.

He drew his knife and was about to wedge it between the mechanical animal's jaws to keep them from pressing tighter.

Too late.

The dog's teeth were sinking deeper and he felt the head begin to swing in a vicious ripping motion . . .

He instinctively raised his knife to the animal's throat and hesitated at the last moment.

This was not an ordinary animal. This was one of the metal dogs that no knife or spear or arrow could penetrate.

The Tree Father's words burst into his mind:

I have always thought of you as my true son. My son, Eric. Promise to keep the knife with you always.

Of course! How could he have forgotten?

This was not *his* knife. It was the jeweled knife that the Tree Father had given him.

He held the blade against the dog's throat and pressed the ruby. He felt the blade sink through metal. As the teeth tore at his shoulder, he slashed the blade down from the creature's throat to it's chest.

It's not working, he thought frantically. I can't stop it from tearing my shoulder apart.

They had been sinking deeper and deeper with the sunlight far above them. Suddenly the dog's eyes glowed with all the brilliance of sunlight. The jaws slackened and Eric pulled his left arm free. He remembered the Tree Father's words:

There is another disease that befalls the metal dogs. It is also caused by water, and yet it is not like the rust disease that lingers. This other disease is quick, as quick as a man's heart can stop when he is old or sick. It is named short-circuit. When it happens, it is called short-circuiting.

And the Tree Father had said this disease would strike a metal dog if it should be struck by a heavy rain or fall into a river. Perhaps the knife wound had finally made the short-circuit disease possible.

At the instant of victory, as the metal dog sank toward the river bottom, Eric tried to pull his knife free. A second flash of light from the mechanical dog's chest burned and numbed his hand so violently that in shock his fingers spread and the knife tumbled from his grasp. It was quickly beyond his vision, falling into the darkness of water below. He wanted to retrieve the knife but now his lungs were burning for air and he had no choice except to thrust toward the surface.

He reached the surface long moments later, gasping for air while his heart pounded. Was Alicia safe? Had she been attacked by other dogs? He searched the cliff, his eyes straining.

Alicia was not there.

With a sinking sensation in his heart, he saw the row of dogs on the cliff.

They had killed Alicia!

And now they would wait for him to swim ashore.

"Eric!"

She was only a yard away, but he had been facing the opposite direction when he surfaced. He took her in his arms briefly and then indicated the river bank.

"Over there. They won't be able to follow us."

A few minutes later when they climbed wearily onto the bank and turned to look at their pursuers, Eric saw the metal dogs turn in unison and head upstream, following the path along the opposite bank.

They'll find a crossing place, he thought, *We've*

64

gained only a few hours . . .

Then, as he still watched, one of the distant pursuers toppled into the river. A second. A third.

The Tree People were swinging from vines, striking the dogs and hurling them into the river. The attack was so swift that the animals did not have time to react. Someone on the opposite bank waved and Eric returned the gesture.

Amazed that others had come forth in his defense, he took Alicia's hand and led her into the jungle. She was tense and shivering as if from shock, but appeared otherwise unharmed.

"My legs feel weak," Alicia said, leaning against him. "Can we rest awhile?"

"You can wait here. And rest." Bushes grew thickly on this side of the river, but they were near a small grassy area. It would be a perfect place for Alicia to wait for him. He led her to the grassy section, and they settled down into what felt like a velvety green fur. "Stay out of sight and you'll be safe. I have to swim to the other side. My spears are there. We will need them."

She looked into his eyes and he had the impression she wanted to be kissed. But as her blue eyes drifted down to his mouth and she moved closer, she saw the scars and blood on his shoulder. "You're hurt," she said softly.

"Not as bad as it could have been. The dog acted as if it didn't want to hurt me."

"But it should be bandaged."

"Not now. Wait until I've come back. The bandages would get wet and might come loose when I swim across the river. I have to go now. We don't want to waste too much time.''

He kissed her on the mouth, briefly but hard, and moved off through the bushes toward the water.

As he swam toward the other bank, he realized this might be his only opportunity to search for the Tree Father's ruby knife. He took a deep breath and dove. Struggling downward, his lungs were burning for air by the time he reached the muddy bottom. He could feel the mud but the light at this depth had dwindled to nothing. He made repeated attempts to find the knife and decided it was futile. He had no way of knowing the exact location where he had dropped the weapon, and the trees on either side of the river shielded enough sunlight that the remaining sun could not penetrate that depth of water.

Reaching the opposite bank and climbing to the top of the cliff, he was surprised to find Karl Springer standing beside his spears.

Karl held the rank of colonel in the Tree People's unofficial army of Archers. Eric had known him for years and they were good friends. Eric privately considered the Archers a relatively useless organization. They had been formed, it was said, to protect everyone. With their bows and arrows, they would have been capable of fending off attackers, but the Tree People had never been attacked in all the centuries of their existence. The Archers seemed independent of the people they were to supposedly defend. They procured their own food by use of their arrows and took care of most of their own needs independently of any other group. They lived in camps separate from the main body, and it seemed to Eric the Archers had usually remained distant, an almost invisible part of the Tree People's society. Recently he had heard nothing at all of the Archers and had forgotten about them until this moment. He remembered now that although they could be incredibly accurate with their arrows, they had proven generally effective against only small animals. Although it was said that an arrow could kill a man instantly, it was comparatively useless against the sturdier structure of tigers. Tragic experience had proven that only a strong thrust from a well-aimed spear could stop a tiger and, therefore, Hunters rarely carried bows and arrows as a weapon.

Karl grinned as Eric approached. "Glad to see you're still in one piece, Eric."

"Thanks." Eric's shoulder ached but he knew from the feel of the wound and long experience that the wound would bleed awhile, coagulate, and then heal properly. If Alicia could bandage them somehow, they would coagulate and heal faster, but there was no need to see one of the doctors for stitching.

"We were maneuvering into position to take the dogs off your trail. I saw the large dog attack and I saw it running through the fields. Faster than the others. Much faster. I believe the Techs have produced a newer and better model."

"Maybe, but that one will not be of any use to them now."

"Your Alicia is unharmed?"

Eric nodded affirmatively and picked up the spears he had dropped so quickly and automatically when the dog first attacked. The spears were held together on a leather strap that fitted over and across his shoulders. He had to adjust carefully to keep the weight of the strap from pulling against his damaged flesh. He knew that swimming to the other side would be difficult with the added weight of spears, but he had no choice. The spears could mean the difference between life and death in the near future.

"You've lost your knife."

"At the bottom of the river somewhere. I tried to find it and couldn't."

Karl unbuckled his sword belt and handed the belt and sheathed sword to Eric. "Take this," he offered. "You'll need it."

Eric was too stunned to move or speak for a moment. It was said there were no more than a dozen swords on the entire planet. The Techs and Guiders at Homebase had the technology to produce swords but had no need for them since they lived within a walled, protected community. The Hunters and Tree People and Archers who had to struggle against every type of animal imaginable could use swords as a tool for survival, but no more than a dozen were in existence. It was said that these had been manufactured long ago by a metalsmith who knew the art of producing and tempering steel. The swords had been passed from father to son and were valued more than any other type of weapon.

Eric's throat felt dry. He said quietly, "Thank you," accepted the sword and strapped it around his waist.

He was about to turn away when a sudden thought struck. "Did you know we would be coming this way? Or—"

"The Tree Father alerted us that you planned to take Alicia. He asked us to protect you. We have wanted to revolt against the Guiders for many years. We needed a cause. We will protect you as much as we can. Now you can continue on to the Valley of the Tigers, and we will wait here for any other trackers that may try to follow your trail. Perhaps you should move on now. We'll have a chance to talk later."

Eric nodded, turned and climbed down the cliff toward the river.

He felt strangely numb inside. He had intended his relationship with Alicia to be a personal and private event that no one except the Tree Father knew. Now Karl was saying his act had been used as the spark to start a full-scale revolution.

Guider Wesley turned off the console and closed his eyes. X-20 had worked excellently, far better than previous models. Until the fall into the river. They had designed the newest model to be waterproof and it had obviously failed.

"Lost it?" Guider Hastings inquired. He sat at the adjoining console, controlling the twelve dogs that had been following the faster X-20.

"Short circuit," Wesley explained. He opened his eyes and blinked rapidly. The screen before him had flashed brilliantly for an instant and then died to emptiness as all the controls became unresponsive. He had witnessed these short circuits several times before. They were ironic in that the visual transmitter was the last of the components to fail and therefore able to transmit the flash that indicated the unit's death.

"Too bad," Hastings said. "Well, it'll give the

Techs some more work. Bromfield keeps insisting on waterproof dogs.''

Wesley rubbed his eyes and turned toward Hastings, wondering how his units were responding.

"Did you get the Hunter named Eric?" Hastings asked casually. Wesley disliked the way some of the Guiders acted as if the Hunters and Herb-Seekers were not even human.

"No. I damaged his arm, that's all." I could have kiled him, Wesley thought. If I could have been more detached and brutal.

"I see him," Hastings said. "He came up for air."

"What happened to Alicia?"

"She dove into the river," Hastings answered, grinning as if pleased that the girl had escaped. "See?"

Wesley rolled his chair over beside Hastings' and studied the console screen. Designed so that one Guider or Tech could simultaneously control a dozen units, the viewscreen was divided into twelve sections. The images as seen through the eyes of the mechanical dogs were nearly identical.

"They're swimming to the other bank," Hastings said absently.

Wesley watched as the pair climbed out of the water. From the distance and angle, he knew Hastings had placed his twelve units on the cliff at the same position where he had attacked Eric with X-20.

"They're looking at us," Hastings added, again absently, as if lost in thought and referring to the mechanical animals as personal extensions. His fingers played on the console keyboard and the top left screen zoomed in on Alicia, the telescopic lenses showing clearly how the wet dress clung to the sensual curves of her body.

"She's all right," Wesley said, noticing there were no signs of injury.

Hastings laughed. "Eric the Hunter should be a lucky man tonight. He should sleep well. My heart's not in it, but I better get those dogs moving. The closest crossover point is miles upstream."

As Wesley watched, Hastings set the dogs in motion once more. But—suddenly—one of the twelve view screens whirled. A second. Then a third. Hastings was paralyzed at the console. Wesley thought, Someone or something is hurling the dogs off the cliff, into the river.

The units were short-circuiting as they struck the water. Hastings, overcoming the initial shock at the unexpected attack, tried to take evasive action. All twelve units expired.

Hastings turned the console off with a swipe of his hand and muttered, "Sonofabitch."

"What happened?"

"They must have planned it. I could only catch glimpses, but the Tree People were swinging from vines and knocking the dogs into the river."

"The Tree People? Helping a Hunter?"

"You know what that means."

"Revolution?"

"It's been brewing for quite a while and the rumors have been stronger and stronger. So it looks as if it's finally happened."

"Are you sure it means a revolution has started?"

"This is the first time anyone has deliberately destroyed twelve of our units."

"Someone will have to tell President Bromfield."

"I can do that," Hastings volunteered.

Wesley studied his companion. Hastings was tall and strong, a handsome man and popular with the women at Homebase. He was intelligent and ambitious in various areas. Some said he wanted the Guider presidency. For one reason or another, it was obvious that Hastings would take delight in informing Bromfield of the new difficulty.

Difficulty? As Wesley watched Hastings leave the room, he mentally rephrased the situation.

As he saw it, revolution was the difficulty, and that was only another word for war.

A war that would engulf the whole planet.

8

Rover, the anteater, lay on its cushion, either asleep or pretending to be. The children had been petting and feeding it ants most of the morning. Its mate, Roverette, had given birth to five small anteaters the previous night. The news had spread like wildfire among the children. In a congratulatory mood, they had been feeding Rover an extra large supply of ants.

Nurse Fay rapped upon her desk, summoning the children to silence.

Thirty boys. The young faces turned toward her desk. A silence fell over the room. Nurse Fay was well-known as the best disciplinarian in the school. She meted punishment swiftly and painfully. The children judged her to be fair. They knew she was soft-hearted and loving beneath the rough and apparently inflexible exterior. So long as they obeyed the rules and did not offend Nurse Fay, they were rewarded with smiles, an affectionate hug, a gentle hand on the shoulder or head. When they broke a rule, Nurse Fay's hand could strike so swiftly as to leave one's cheek stinging for an hour.

"This is the first day of your new subject, history," Nurse Fay began slowly. "I know that many of you have already heard things about our history from older boys, or from talking with the Techs or Guiders. But this class is the place where we begin your formal and orderly education on the subject.

"We can start with the very basics. As you all know, we came from earth on a ship named The U.S.S. Corsair. When the ship arrived, it contained three hundred men and three nurses. The Corsair was on its way to take part in a terrible intergalactic war when its radios and some other equipment were damaged by an explosion. The Corsair was forced to land here and our ancestors named this planet Earth Two. I'm sure all of you have heard those details before."

Nurse Fay paused, glancing down at her handwritten notes. She raised a finger. "But how many of you know that on our original planet, Earth, there was a custom called marriage?"

Glancing up, she saw that every hand was raised except Irving's. Irving was one of her problem children. He tended to be a loner and basically unresponsive.

"Very good. Now." She waited until the hands were lowered. "Will someone explain what the custom of marriage is?"

Fewer hands were raised this time—only about half the class. She chose Johnny.

75

He rose. "Guider Falcon told me that marriage was a system whereby one man lived with one woman. He said on earth the terms were husband and wife." Johnny hesitated. "Rover and Roverette are married, husband and wife, in a way, aren't they?'

"Yes. Very good." She saw Johnny sitting down in his chair again. Without warning, she found her eyes filling with tears. Why? Johnny had once more referred to a conversation with Guider Falcon. It seemed that Guider Falcon was quite often having little talks with Johnny. Once she had seen them sitting together on a bench outside Homebase by the small lake. They had skipped small stones across the smooth watery surface. Falcon, befitting the dignity required of a Guider, had sat on the bench and thrown the stones casually. Johnny had been running back and forth, bursting with boyish enthusiasm to skip a stone completely across the lake so it would land high and dry on the other side.

Did Guider Falcon suspect that Johnny was his son? Is that why he spent so much time with him, much more than he spent with the other boys?

She ran the tip of her tongue across her lips. She swallowed. She took a deep slow breath.

Her eyes were so filled with tears that all the faces of her class were blurred. Her heart began to beat more rapidly. She knew that one of the boys in the class was her son. She had narrowed it down that far. Which one? It could be Johnny, or Irving, or Mark, or—

As the tears completely filled her eyes, all the boyish faces seemed to run together. Thirty molded into one. And, once more, she felt that strange heart-bursting fantastic sensation, the sensation that *all* the children were hers.

9

Swimming across the river with the added weight of spears and sword, Eric's arms and legs began to feel leaden, and there came a time when he doubted he could continue.

Alicia was waiting at the edge of the river and helped him into the small clearing. She removed her blouse and carefully used it to dry his chest. She said, "I have a bandage ready," and, as Eric rested and tried to gather his strength, she began tying strips of cloth around his wound. He guessed she must have taken her undergarment and torn it into suitable lengths and tied them together to form a usable bandage.

She said she had seen him talking to someone on the other side of the river and he explained the man was Karl Springer, colonel of the Archers.

"He gave me his sword," Eric added, touching the hilt of the sword as if in demonstration, but Alicia's eyes did not waver from her work.

"Did you tell him we would take this route? Is that how he and the others were here in time to help us?"

"I didn't tell anyone of my plans except the Tree Father. I thought he wouldn't tell anyone."

"I've heard people speak of the Tree Father," Alicia interrupted. "He sounds kindly . . . and interesting."

"He said he would like to meet you someday."

"Really?" Her face brightened. "Could we go there now? I'd love to meet him."

Eric hesitated. Alicia sounded almost childlike. Her suggestion was not practical at all. He wondered if living in one of the towers for years had caused her to have an unrealistic attitude about life. Didn't she realize they had both narrowly escaped death less than an hour ago? Couldn't she understand that the villages would be watched closely by the Techs and Guiders?

"This wouldn't be a good time," Eric said gently. "Later. First we must go to the Valley of Tigers. No one will follow us there."

She finished bandaging his chest. "What is the Valley of Tigers like?"

Eric described their future home, emphasizing the good features and playing down the bad.

"Is it far from here?" Alicia asked.

"It isn't far but we'll have to cut through the jungle. It wouldn't be safe to follow the paths along the river. The trackers could intercept us at any point and it would be easy, too easy, for them to follow our trail. Progress through the jungle will be slow

79

but we'll be able to move much faster than anyone else. As a matter of fact, I don't see how the metal dogs could follow us at all."

"How long will it take to reach the Valley of Tigers?"

Eric was evasive, "I have a place for us to rest on our way there. And, even before we come to the resting place I've prepared, there is another place we can rest awhile. Have you heard of places in the jungle called the sundra?"

"I've heard of them. Places where nothing grows, where the ground is like a mixture of sand and salt. I've heard the Guiders discuss them and argue about what caused them."

Eric, too, had heard various theories about the origin of the sundra. Each was an exact circle several hundred feet in diameter. Nothing at all grew within the circles, and since they were numerous, miles apart, and formed a series of straight lines in different directions, it had been argued that the sundra were navigational aides installed by an alien race that had visited Earth Two long before the arrival of the Corsair.

Others argued that the sundras were the equivalent of landing fields, and still others argued that they were relics of a civilization native to Earth Two, perhaps areas cleared as living space for communities.

Alicia had finished bandaging his chest. "How do the bandages feel? They're not too tight, are they?"

He moved his arm in a circle to test the restriction. "Good," he complimented.

She smiled, her blue eyes studying him. "Do you know how the sundras were named?"

"No."

"On earth there were treeless plains in the arctic regions called the tundra. Since the areas with no trees and no vegetation of any kind, on this planet, are located in a warm, sunny region, someone thought to name them sundra. Do you think they were made by aliens?"

"I believe it's a possibility. You've heard of the Zeanorian spaceships that have been found?"

She nodded affirmatively. "I know that four or five have been found. Why do you ask?"

"I discovered an alien starship that no one else knows about. It will be our resting place between the sundra, and Valley of Tigers."

"How did you find it? I've always wanted to see one of the Zeanorian ships, but people at Homebase are never allowed to visit any other part of the colony. Did you stumble across the ship by accident or—"

Glancing at the position of the sun in the sky and realizing they would have to start moving soon before they were caught in the jungle at nightfall, he said, "I'll tell you later. We should start moving again. It isn't too far to the sundra."

They kissed and Eric found himself slipping his arms around Alicia, holding her tighter and tighter. He felt her arms on his back and the pressure of her fingernails biting into his flesh—lightly but still a very definite sensation. The kiss went on and on. He felt aroused and knew she was too. It would have been so easy to make love with her then. He wanted

81

to. Yet he knew it would sap their strength and make them languorous.

When the kiss slowly ended on a reluctant note, he rose, unable to look at her. Tonight, he thought. Tonight. It would be like the ancient honeymoon ritual on earth.

Minutes later they were moving off into the jungle and the growth became thicker and thicker. It was, Eric saw, much more dense than his last journey in this direction. He had expected to clear a path for both of them with only his knife. Now even with Kurt's sword the journey became incredibly tedious.

He had to slash with the sword at vines as thick as his fingers and tree-like growths the size of his wrist. The sun bore down on them mercilessly, and he began pouring sweat from every inch of his body. Slashing with the sword was painful since it soon tore apart the wounds that had only just started to heal. Before long the sweat from his body was penetrating the fabric of the bandages and soaking into the raw flesh with the sensation of hot pokers.

Alicia followed uncomplaining, but he could see the agonized expression on her face that she could not conceal. Her dress clung to her sweat-damp body and her arms and legs were covered with countless scratches and abrasions.

I'll make it up to her somehow, he thought, and plowed on through the jungle.

There came a period when the haze of exhaustion and pain gave all his surroundings a sense of unreality. He moved on like an image in a pain-wracked nightmare. Twice he climbed to the peaks of the tallest trees to be certain they were headed toward the sundra between the river and the alien starship. He could not see direct evidence of the sundra but, each time, was able to discern a seeming valley in the thick jungle—an absence of growth that had to be the sundra.

He did not speak. His mind was too numb for even the simplest conversation. Leading the way, he tried to make the path as comfortable as possible for Alicia, but still he could see this was a difficult and torturous trek for her. She screamed once and he whirled to see one of the gray, spidery creatures the size of a man's fist had landed on her shoulder. She was shivering violently with fear but was otherwise paralyzed. He brushed the creature from her and killed it with the sword.

Minutes later they reached the edge of the sundra and burst through a last wall of jungle to the freedom of empty space. An expanse of white sand stretched before them in a circle for hundreds of feet. Eric turned toward Alicia and said, "The hardest part is past now. From here to the alien starship is less than one-fourth the distance we've already covered. We'll be able to rest and still reach the ship before night." As he studied her, he saw she was sweating and much paler. He added anxiously, "Are you all right?"

"The spider was the worst part," she said, forcing a smile. "Yes. I'm all right."

He was about to say they should eat some of the fruit that grew on vines near the edge of the sundra, but the words froze in his mouth as he watched her close her eyes and crumple to the sand. He knelt beside her and rolled her over onto her back.

"Alicia?" She was so limp, so lifeless. "Alicia?" He reached for her wrist to check for a pulse but a blackness exploded in the center of his skull. He felt himself falling, wondering what had struck him. Then his thoughts ended in the darkness of an oblivion.

10

President Glenn Bromfield felt more tense than he had at any other time in his life. During the past months, it seemed everything had started to go wrong. A few minutes ago the climax had arrived. Hastings had obviously enjoyed bringing the news that a revolution appeared to be underway.

He closed his eyes a moment and settled deeper into the warm water. He tried to consciously relax each muscle. The four attendants were lathering his body with soap. Ordinarily he would have been aroused by the sensation of their hands, but now he could think only of the news that Hastings had brought. Twelve regular models of tracker dogs destroyed. The improved experimental model out of commission also.

At times he felt as if everyone at Homebase wanted to revolt against his leadership. There had been rumors of impeachment, a rumor previously unheard of on Earth Two. Now, he wondered, since a revolution by the Tree People had started, would he be blamed? And could that be used as an impetus to eventually remove him from office?

He knew he would have to consult Diana, his First Cohabitor, and Rachel, his Second Cohabitor. They had been his advisors for many years and he respected their opinions, secretly considering each to be more intelligent than himself—and more knowledgeable in the mechanics of their society.

I'll contact them and ask their advice as soon as I finish the bath, he decided.

Having made a decision to seek help rather than act on his own initiative, he relaxed, but opened his eyes to study the attendants.

Each girl was nude and two were in the tub also. Jennifer, eighteen, had become an electronics Tech, extremely competent. Loris, seventeen, was studying astronomy. Marla, sixteen, had chosen psychology as her major subject and Dawn, fifteen, had selected sociology. They were all healthy and beautiful, strong, intelligent, carefully selected from the elite of their colony.

Glenn had originated the system of attendants whereby the president of the colony was able to spend many hours with the young, virginal girls at Homebase in every type of relationship from bathing, to eating together, to relaxation periods and socializing—everything, that is, short of sleeping together and sexual contact. He enjoyed the system because it became a means of familiarization whereby he was able to become acquainted with the available girls and selected the ones he wanted to involve in courtship.

After the two in the tub finished scrubbing and rinsing his body, he began lathering their bodies. Blonde-haired Jennifer sat with her eyes closed, enjoying the sensual contact. Loris began scrubbing her own body as if too impatient to wait her turn. Standing outside the tub with towels, Marla appeared bored with the whole procedure while Dawn watched avidly, apparently aroused by this nude encounter. Glenn Bromfield had decided several days ago that Jennifer and Dawn would make good cohabitors whereas Loris and Marla were not sufficiently sexual to become good partners. At least in his own judgment and according to his own preferences.

After he finished rinsing the girls' bodies, he rose from the tub and accepted one of the towels. He quickly dried himself and nodded to Jennifer and Dawn to indicate he wanted to talk to them in the adjoining dressing room. They followed him eagerly and Dawn locked the door. Soundlessly the girls and Glenn Bromfield repeated a sensuous contact they had originated a few weeks previously, a physical relationship in which they remained nude, standing together, arms around each other, kissing, touching, caressing, sliding body against body, hands moving with greater and greater passion until the three-way union became a form of group masturbation. Jennifer and Dawn were both deft when using their hands. During previous experiments, Glenn Bromfield had found Loris and Marla to be mechanical, aroused, but with no sensuality or sense of rhythm. Jennifer's eyes were glazed with passion, and her mouth fell apart as she gasped when she climaxed beneath his touch. Dawn began moaning softly and Bromfield held her tighter until she groaned and went limp with her release. The contact completed, the three kissed one last time and began dressing hurriedly. Bromfield knew he might be criticized for his actions, but not severely, since he had not penetrated either of the girls. Masturbation, considered a mild perversion or mild evil during the dark ages on Earth, had become acceptable in Earth's society and even more acceptable on Earth Two where it had become a customary method of relieving tensions.

After he finished dressing, Bromfield moved on into the office section of the presidential quarters where he asked Felicia, the secretary, to summon Diana and Rachel immediately, telling them it was of the utmost importance.

"It shouldn't take long to locate them," Felicia said, turning toward the intercom that would send other presidential aides on the task. "Where shall I ask them to meet you?"

"In the conference room." He went through the doorway to the next room which contained a long table with twenty-two chairs, while the corners of the room were furnished with comfortable chairs arranged in close circles. Bromfield had always been restless in nature and adjustment after his election had been difficult. One of the hardest elements had been the long hours required to sit and study reports. After a short time, out of restlessness, he had taken to dictating to Felicia in the conference room, simply as a change of pace during the days that had started to seem incredibly long. It was here, he remembered suddenly, that Felicia had seduced him. He had decided not to have a sexual relationship with her as it might interfere with his duties as president. She, on the other hand, must have been curious and made her own decision. Shortly after the inauguration, when he finished dictating communications one day, she had quickly undressed without any sort of preamble or foreplay, and, when he stared at her naked body, stunned, too surprised to move or speak, she had smiled at him and whispered, "It is inevitable, isn't it?" She had also whispered something about not being able to stand the suspense, but he had not been able to pay much attention to the words because she had started to undress him and, moments later, settled on his lap.

"Are you asleep, Glenn?"

He opened his eyes and smiled at Diana and Rachel as they slipped into chairs. He realized he had become drowsy while reminiscing about the experience with Felica.

"I suppose you've guessed why I wanted to talk to you?" Bromfield opened.

Diana, tall, slender, dark-haired, nodded solemnly. "You're in trouble. You want our help." Diana wore a pair of slacks and a long-sleeved blouse. At the beginning of their relationsip, he had mentioned he didn't like slacks and had stated his preference quite often during their cohabitation. In defiance and to deliberately annoy him, it seemed she quite often wore slacks or very long skirts. He had once been intrigued by the mystery of her body since she kept it so concealed. She had a beautifully

89

shaped face with dark eyes that matched her dark hair. She had been described as tall and cool by other men, and Bromfield had decided it was very accurate although succinct. Her coolness bordered on frigidity in his own estimation. It was ironic that she headed the small clothes industry on Earth Two and had invented methods of fabricating and weaving both synthetic materials and native forms of vegetation and fur. Everyone said that Diana was a genius in her own way, and Bromfield agreed, but she lacked many of the features he had always considered womanly and feminine.

You're in trouble. You want our help. Bromfield resisted the temptation to respond angrily. Diana had never ceased to be of help, but during the past year she had become more and more taunting.

Fighting for self control, he answered, "Our colony is in trouble. I do want your suggestions. Have you heard—"

Rachel raised her eyebrow. "The revolution? Word has spread everywhere. Every detail. If it could have been contained . . . Too late. Every person in Homebase that has been discontent for one reason or another will start to look for a way to join the existing revolution or utilize the confusion to his or her advantage. I am afraid there will be sabotage by negligence and by outright acts."

Turning toward Rachel as she spoke, Bromfield realized he had chosen as his cohabitors two women who were as different as night and day. Rachel, blonde-haired and voluptuous, always wore mid-thigh skirts along with short-sleeved or sleeveless blouses. She was warm and sensual, open, loving, womanly, and feminine without being subservient. She worked as a volunteer nurse in several departments, caring for the babies with nameless fathers, working in the nursery and also in the kindergarten. It was typical of Rachel to not seek acclaim of any sort, to be content with the personal satisfaction of helping others.

"Do you have any suggestions, Rachel?"

"You must attempt to find Alicia and Eric immediately. They have to be killed as an example. If they are not, you will have numerous other desertions and acts of destruction."

Bromfield was silent as he studied Rachel. So strange to hear her speak of death so easily, the woman that had been so loving to him and the mother of three of his children. He remembered how tender she had appeared when holding their babies. And now she spoke of murdering Alicia and Eric as if she were speaking of animals rather than human beings. It was a response he would have expected of Diana rather than Rachel.

"I would prefer not to kill Alicia," Bromfield said. "I was thinking of pursuing both until they are captured and possibly eliminating the Hunter Eric during the encounter to make it seem he had to be killed as a means of self-defense. I would prefer to have Alicia return to Homebase. And convince her that she should make a public statement that Eric forced her to go with him."

"And if she should insist on testifying that she left with Eric willingly?"

"That would be foolish on her part, but if she did take that course, then I think the proper action would be to confine her. I regret we had to track down and execute the defecting Tech several days ago. I believe that policy has been detrimental to our image."

"And what would you do to a defector? Bring him back and slap his wrist?"

Bromfield did not reply to the question. He sat quietly and studied Rachel. She was a woman but somehow colder and more brutal than most men. It had taken him a long time to realize the truth, and, delving into the records, he had discovered one day that she had been instrumental in establishing the death penalty for defectors. He had difficulty visualizing her role in their society but could visualize it partly when he imagined her as the equivalent of a tigress, loving toward her cubs but vicious toward any element of change that threatened them or herself.

"Diana?"

"I think immediate action is necessary. Every available tracker should be put to use and assembly of new units should be accelerated. If you persist in your idea of returning Alicia to Homebase alive, then I think it would be effective if she were to state that Eric in essence kidnapped her. If she does not make that kind of statement, she would have to be imprisoned as an example."

"You talk as if we should wage a full scale war against the Tree People."

"I feel any move we make from this moment on will be defensive. The revolution—the war—is already in motion. At this point even an attack by our forces is nothing more than a counter move."

"Is there any way we can restore peace?"

Diana laughed softly. "Peace? Glenn, this colony has not been at peace since our starship crashed here. We have always been in conflict—against our alien environment—one sex against the other—each rank and class struggling for dominance. After the divisions a few centuries ago, the Techs and Guiders of Homebase have always been in conflict with the Hunters and Tree People."

Bromfield remained silent awhile, thinking. "What is your estimate of how this war will end?"

Diana's expression changed to one of sadness. "We have a technological advantage but they are stronger, more cunning, more desperate. I feel the deaths will be almost equal on each side and will continue equally until the conflict ends, with only a handful of survivors—unless something happens to terminate the revolution before it progresses that far."

"Then you think victory would be long and difficult to obtain?"

"I am not certain we will emerge as the victors."

"But we have the technological advantage—the science and the machines—"

"And they outnumber us by ten to one," Diana warned.

11

After class dismissal, Nurse Fay went out to the pen behind the small school building. Many of her students were there and also four girls from Nurse Stella's class. The boys had apparently arrived first because they were at the section of fence closest to Roverette and her babies. Because of the regulation that boys and girls had to maintain a separation of at least three yards, except on designated special occasions such as The Family Birthday Party and The Family Christmas, the girls were forced to remain at a section of fence where they had a poor view of the female anteater and her offspring.

Boys were trained to give in to girls' wishes. It was evident that the girls wanted to stand at the fence closest to Roverette, so they could have a good view of the new babies. The boys, however, were clever enough to pretend they did not see the girls. They hung onto the fence, eyes straight ahead.

"Ain't they small?" someone whispered in awe.

Nurse Fay shuddered at the word ain't and opened her mouth but then reminded herself that she was outside the classroom and it wasn't exactly fair to pursue the children on their free time, correcting their English. She closed her mouth and set her lips firmly.

It was Roger's day to return Rover to the pen. She watched as he fumbled with the lock and let Rover walk inside. He held the leash above the gate as he closed and locked it. Then he worked the end of the leash down to knee level by passing it from one hand to another through the openings in the fence mesh. Gently tugging on the leash until he could reach the clasp at Rover's collar, he unfastened it.

Rover wandered over to where Roverette lay. Almost wearily, Nurse Fay thought, like someone returning to his room after a day's work. Perhaps putting up with the pettings and games and general attention of thirty boys all day was the equivalent of a day's work for an anteater.

He nuzzled Roverette briefly, then carefully walked to stand near his new additions. To Nurse Fay it seemed that he studied them with a mixture of curiosity, affection, and bewilderment. She could imagine his relatively primitive brain grappling with the question, How did this happen? She was pleased and surprised when Rover's long tongue licked gently across each of the babies' backs. It was as if he had kissed them! The boys and girls murmured.

"Seen Johnny?"

Nurse Fay jumped involuntarily. It was Guider Falcon.

"No. I'm not sure where he is."

"Look! One of them is starting to walk!" a child shouted.

A baby anteater was struggling to rise to its feet. It kept collapsing but persisted in its efforts. It remained on its feet a little longer each time it tried.

"Nurse Fay, don't you think your boys have spent long enough at this side of the fence?"

"Oh. Yes, Nurse Stella. I'm sorry." She lied, "I'm sorry. I didn't see your girls waiting." She said in a sharp voice, "Boys! That's enough! Move on so the girls can see!"

The boys departed quickly and yet somehow managed to convey both reluctance and defiance. The girls gathered at the vacant vantage point were soon ooohhing and aaahhing.

Nurse Fay had stepped back. Guider Falcon moved back with her, frowning thoughtfully. They were beyond earshot of the girls and Nurse Stella. She glanced rapidly in each direction and saw no one else was near.

"You think he's yours?" she asked in a whisper, her heart beating rapidly.

"What?"

"Johnny. You think he's your son?"

"Why do you—?"

She took a deep breath. As Nurses and Guiders, they were not permitted to know the identities of the children's parents. This was a carefully guarded secret with the supposed result, that, as a Nurse or a Guider or a Tech, you would never know which boy or girl was your own—thus you would treat them all as yours. The idea had worked for some hundreds of years. It was technically illegal to try to identify your child. Punishments could be given for the crime against society, the sin of wanting to know your flesh and blood. Yet it was a crime that many indulged in, some casually, some relentlessly.

"Let's not play games with each other," she said. "I'm Johnny's teacher, remember? I've lost count of the times he's said Guider Falcon told me this and Guider Falcon told me that. I'm sure none of the other boys paid any attention but I noticed. You'd have to be having a considerable number of talks for him to quote you so much."

"I like the boy," Falcon said defensively. "Is that a crime? He's a good kid, so I spend a lot of time with him."

"I saw the two of you at the lake, skipping stones across the water." As soon as she said it, she realized it was not much evidence. Many of the Guiders spent time with the boys. Some had preferences.

Falcon laughed. "Skipping stones! I've done that with dozens of boys! We're supposed to be like fathers and big brothers! I've skipped stones with dozens—"

"You haven't," Nurse Fay said. "I've been walking down to the lake almost every day for years and I've never seen you there with any boy except Johnny."

He gripped her arm. He was hurting her and his teeth were gritting. He said harshly, "You looking for trouble? You want to get me disbarred as a Guider?"

The truth shocked her. He was afraid she was out to ruin him! There were some Nurses who were such fanatics that they delighted in having Guiders disbarred because of the slightest infractions of rules. A disbarred Guider became a faceless Worker, forced to perform the most menial duties. Guiders were powerful, yet they had to always be careful and defensive.

"Oh no! I'm not trying to cause trouble—" Once more she felt tears filling her eyes. She was trembling. She knew her nerves were on edge. Falcon was staring at her face, his eyes following the trickle of tears down her cheeks. "I—I'm doing the same thing, trying to find my son. I'm sure he's in my class. I've traced him that far."

"You're upset," Falcon said. "Let's go in the classroom. You don't want Nurse Stella and her girls to see you like this."

She nodded agreement. He took her hand. Luckily they were near the corner of the school building and were able to slip out of sight in a few seconds. She went up the stairs and into the classroom, partially blinded by her tears. She rubbed her knuckles at them.

Falcon closed the door behind them. The classroom was empty and silent.

"Are you going to be all right?" he asked. When she looked up at him, she saw that no trace of anger or suspicion remained on his face. By her admission that she had been trying to identify her son, she had admitted she was a criminal. If she had him disbarred as a Guider, he could have her disbarred as a Nurse. She had placed them in a position where they could have mutual trust.

"I'll be all right. My nerves haven't been too

good recently."

He was standing very close. He rubbed the tips of his fingers at the tears on her cheeks. "Nerves? You've been feeling tense?"

"Yes. I don't know—"

"Maybe you've been working too hard."

"Could be."

He was smiling at her, obviously trying to cheer her. His eyes brightened. "Maybe you haven't been having enough—" He faltered. She felt her cheeks flush.

Leaning forward, he brushed his lips against hers. It was a sensuous, light, teasing kiss.

He said, "Remember?"

"Yes." It had been a long time ago. They had been intimate, but then, somehow, they had drifted apart.

His body became suddenly rigid, his eyes widened. "My God." She was startled. He whispered in awe, "Suppose Johnny is our son!"

12

As Eric regained consciousness, he had the strange sensation that hours had passed. He could not understand the period of blackness. He had blacked out a few times from loss of blood, once from exhaustion, and twice from being struck on the head. This time had not been like any of his previous experiences.

Alicia's eyes fluttered open. She quickly moved into a sitting position. "W-What happened? Did I faint?"

"Something happened. I'm not sure what. I was out for awhile too."

Alicia rubbed her forehead and said, "I have the strangest feeling I slept for hours."

"I had that same sensation of hours having passed. It must be so, judging from the position of the sun. We should stay here tonight, I think. Otherwise we'd find ourselves traveling through the jungle after dark.''

Alicia shuddered. "I wouldn't want that. It's bad enough during the day.''

"Let's move over there where we'll be in the shade.''

She followed him along the edge of the sundra to a position where the wall of jungle shaded them from the last rays of sunlight. While she rested, he picked a handful of fruit for them to eat. They sat watching the sun disappear on the horizon.

"You promised you'd tell me how you found the alien ship,'' Alicia reminded him.

He finished eating a piece of fruit and said, "I can't remember the exact year it happened, but the events are still crystal clear in my memory. I had some bad luck—the worst kind.

"Three tigers attacked me simultaneously, and I only had three spears that day. I managed to kill the first two, but the third spear only wounded the last tiger.'' Eric grinned at the memory. "He was hurting bad and wanted to chew me into little pieces. He kept charging and I had no choice but to retreat. I retreated into the jungle. I went into the thickest section I knew. I hadn't been in there before, only on the outskirts, but I had seen it was so thick a man couldn't walk in there—or a tiger. I knew the tiger either couldn't follow, or he'd be moving slower than myself. I had my knife to cut my way through the vines and other kinds of growth. He had his paws and nose. That's all. I'd glanced over my shoulder sometimes and saw him blundering along, each time a little bit further behind.

"So my idea turned out to be a good one. It

worked. It became a struggle just to move a yard, and I knew I might be crossing territory that no man had ever crossed before. After awhile I couldn't hear or see the tiger. Then I had to worry about such things as being lost and starving to death or bumping into something else that might be hungry. With only a knife to protect myself. I knew there were—"

He caught himself as he was about to say he knew of the huge pythons in the jungle. He had often heard stories of the giant snakes with bodies anywhere from two to four feet thick and twenty to forty feet in length. If Alicia had not heard of them there was no need to frighten her, since the odds were against their encountering any pythons. He started again, "I knew there were some small animals in the jungle that could cause trouble, so I wanted to find a piece of wood to make a crude spear.

"I was about to give up hope of finding anything worthwhile when I saw the smooth surface of the alien starship. The jungle was so thick it was right at my feet before I noticed it, and even then I could only see small sections through the vines and leaves.

"I had heard of the other ships that had been found, so I knew roughly what to expect. I searched until I found an entrance. I explored the starship and decided not to tell anyone. And I haven't told anyone. Except you. You're the first person I've ever mentioned it to."

"Why didn't you tell someone?" Alicia asked. She had been intensely interested in the story and now leaned forward, eager to hear his answer. "If I had found something like that, I'd have wanted to tell everyone."

"Because I heard the story of the Hunter who discovered one of the alien starships and a tribe of Herb-Seekers somehow took it away from him to use as their home. I was afraid another tribe might take over the ship somehow if they knew about it."

They were sitting very close with their mouths only a few inches apart. Something in her eyes changed and he knew she wanted to be kissed. Her mouth came apart—moist and hungry. His heart began to beat faster as they kissed, arms gliding around each other. They were alone and rested, and he knew they would make love only minutes from now. She moved against him with a body as hungry as her mouth. He unbuttoned her dress and pulled it apart so he could caress the sensuous body and feel the ripe mounds of breasts with nipples as hard as small pebbles. He felt Alicia's hands working on his clothing. She unbuckled the belt that now held the empty knife sheath. He moved a hand down, sliding it down over the flat expanse of her stomach to the furry nest between her thighs. They were still kissing when they glided together. He hadn't wanted it this way. He had wanted their honeymoon night to be at the alien starship where they'd have a chance to bathe first. But it was happening now, unplanned but borne of necessity. He entered in a smooth plunge, pounding, pounding . . . Part of his mind said to be gentle because he loved and didn't want to hurt her and that she was now his equivalent of a wife, but the lustful animal in his nature wanted to be savage, brutal, pound away until she cried out in a mixture of pain and joy.

Her heart beat faster as they kissed. She felt his hands on her body, exploring while she kept her eyes closed. It was hard to believe they were actually here, alone, about to make love. She felt as if they were passing through a dream.

The weekend with Eric had been wonderful. He had been so inexperienced and had frankly admitted that she was his first woman. She had taught him how to kiss, but there had been no need to teach the rest. He had performed them instinctively and wonderfully. She had orgasmed—the first time with a man. All the other men before Eric had seemed like nothing.

When he appeared in her tower and asked her to leave with him, she had decided to say no and wondered how to tell him. The thought had occurred that the best way would be to say it would be impossible for her to leave Homebase, impossible to give up the only way of life she had ever known.

But then he had taken her in his arms and kissed her and she had found herself clinging to him desperately, and, as if watching from another room, heard herself say, "I'll go with you."

The thought of spending every night with him had seemed wonderful. A chance too magnificent to pass by. If she had refused to go, the lonely nights would have been unbearable. It seemed so strange to think they were now exercising that ancient custom on earth called marriage.

Holding Alicia in his arms, Eric wished he could freeze time and make this moment last forever. He began to move more slowly, wishing to stretch the sensation out as long as possible. Once more he had the feeling there was nothing better, nothing more pleasurable, than the mating of a man and woman.

Alicia clutched him as she shuddered with her release. He climaxed a moment later and they lay in each other's arms until Alicia fell asleep. He felt his eyes closing as sleep drew nearer.

The three moons rose in the sky and the moonlight glittered on the Tree Father's ruby knife.

13

"The new model X-20 was faster than the older models," Wesley said. "Performance was at an extremely high level, but it did not prove to be waterproof as we'd hoped. It short-circuited moments after it struck the water."

This was the first technical conference that had been called after the outbreak of the revolution. The small conference room was packed wall-to-wall with people. Wesley felt uncomfortable and wished he could simply get up and leave. Crowds on Earth Two were rare, but whenever he encountered them in the past he had felt very uncomfortable and felt worse than ever now because this was the largest crowd he had been involved in. Every seat was taken and men and women were standing behind the rows of chairs.

Halliday, the Tech in charge of engineering for the mechanical dogs, cleared his throat and said, "I don't doubt that X-20 did short-circuit, but I have some doubts as to why. Our testings of this tracker in the lab were extensive. We kept X-20 submerged in a tank of water for twenty-four hours and kept it moving nearly continuously while we simultaneously made endurance and stress checks. X-20 passed that test with flying colors. Do you know what that means? It was underwater for a whole day!" He shrugged to show his puzzlement. "Then, suddenly, we give it a test in the field, it is made operational and moments after it is in the water, it short-circuits. I am tempted to believe the Hunter somehow created the leak that made the short circuit possible."

"I cannot imagine how the Hunter or anyone else could have done that," Wesley stated. "The Hunters and Tree People do not have weapons capable of penetrating metal."

"True."

"X-20 was not completely metal," another Tech argued. "The joints in its legs were covered with the new flexiskin we began manufacturing a few months ago. Isn't it possible that the Hunter could have used his knife to sever the flexiskin at a joint and thereby caused X-20 to take in water which in turn caused it to short-circuit?"

"I doubt that," Hastings argued. "Past experience has shown that the Hunters and Tree People are ignorant of how the trackers function. We've always been careful to retrieve each tracker that became inoperable. They haven't had any of the dogs to study—and we haven't been giving them classes on operation."

Three or four of those present broke into laughter at the remark. President Bromfield did not even smile and in fact frowned as his stern, gray eyes swept around the room.

The laughter died away quickly and someone said, "Isn't it possible that the flexiskin accidentally broke at a joint during the beginning of the trial run and therefore, when X-20 was submerged in the water, it short-circuited because of the break in flexiskin?"

"That is a possibility."

"Is it really important how the new model failed?"

"Yes. Because of the revolution we have to step up production of trackers. We have a dozen regular models to replace already. Who knows what the rate of loss will be? We have to decide if the X-20 model is worthwhile. The consensus of opinion is that the extra speed is valuable but not worth the extra cost if speed is the only asset over the previous models. Waterproofing was intended to be the great bonus. I feel we have to learn why X-20 failed."

"How can we learn what caused X-20 to fail when it sits at the bottom of a river in what is now, technically speaking, enemy territory?"

"There is only one way to gather the information. We'll have to send a scouting party to retrieve the tracker."

"Do you think it's worth the risk?"

"Absolutely."

"We could lose some of our members."

"So far the Hunters or Tree People have not killed anyone. They've destroyed some trackers, that's all. There is no guarantee they would kill members of a scout party. If the party is careful, it might get in and out of the enemy territory undetected.''

President Bromfield thought, And if they are detected we will learn if this is what our ancestors would call a shooting war. Aloud he said, "I agree with the logic of sending a scouting party. Any volunteers?''

About one-fourth of the men and women in the room raised their hands. Bromfield made a list of ten names.

It was a strange list. Some of the people were included because of their technical ability. Others were listed since they were strong and physically competent to serve as the brawn of the expedition. Some were deadwood and others were people Bromfield simply disliked.

The deadwood and the unfavored ones were on the list because he felt certain the scout party would be attacked and eliminated.

14

Eric stared at the knife until his eyes ached.

It can't be here. I lost it in the river.

He reached out with a hand and touched the hilt. It was real, not a figment of his imagination.

Magic?

When the Tree Father first demonstrated the knife's power to penetrate metal, Eric had thought it must be some form of magic.

But the Tree Father had said, not precisely magic. However, it is a form of science we are not familiar with.

How could the knife return to its sheath from the bottom of the river?

He gradually drifted into a half sleep with Alicia still in his arms. When the morning sun began warming their bodies, Alicia opened her eyes, smiled, and kissed him on the mouth. They made love again. Later Eric explained how he had lost the ruby knife in the river and that it had somehow magically returned to its sheath. He remembered last night she had unbuckled his knife belt.

"Was the Tree Father's knife in the sheath when you—"

She nodded yes. "I didn't think to mention it because you hadn't said anything about losing it."

The knife had returned during their blackout, he reasoned. There was no logical explanation but he could see no point in pondering the matter too long. He picked some more fruit for their breakfast and led the way through the jungle once more. The growth was thicker than the first leg of the journey but this portion was shorter and they soon reached the alien starship. Since the bottom half was buried in the ground and the top half was covered with the thick jungle vegetation, it was nearly invisible at a distance of only a few yards.

Alicia paused at the entrance and appeared fearful.

"Don't be afraid," Eric said. He went in first and lit a candle.

Alicia followed hesitantly, studying her surroundings warily but growing ever more at ease as Eric lit one candle after another.

She shivered. "I know it's not a cave in the ordinary sense of the word but I've read stories of places like this on earth, places called caves. I read that bears hibernated in them, bears that could tear a person apart with its teeth or claws. And snakes . . ."

"There are no bears or snakes here," Eric assured her. "The people who created this ship were much like ourselves—and died a long time ago.''

He closed the outer door, locked it, then led the way deeper into the ship, lighting candles as they moved along. Alicia became more and more relaxed as he explained the purpose of each room. Directly beyond the first compartment was one that he had set aside for a supply of spears and knives. Some tiger skins were stored there also and Alicia seemed impressed by the number.

In the next room, Eric showed Alicia the supply of food he had gathered—mostly fruits and nuts that did not perish rapidly. He had built a crude table with two chairs and, Alicia, studying the furnishings and food, said with a soft smile, ''I like your kitchen.''

Eric, too serious-minded to notice the teasing tone in her voice, explained solemnly, ''There is enough food and water here to last a month—if we wanted to stay that long. But I am sure we will only want to stay overnight, or a day at the most.''

They went on to the next compartment.

''This is what I call the storage room,'' Eric explained with a casual wave of his hand. ''I brought all the alien machines here.''

''Have you tried to learn what they're for?''

''No. How could I understand them and what good would it do?''

Eric had thought Alicia would give the room only a casual glance but she went inside, picking up one object after another, studying each with wonder.

''Did you know how the Zeanorians were given that name by our people?'' Alicia asked.

''No.''

She held one of the objects before his eyes. "See the small printing? It's in their language but the letters resemble ours'. Z-E-A-N-O-R-I-A. See? The Z is very much like our English Z but the O is solid. What someone designated as their equivalent of our A does not have the crossbar. The E has a couple of extra arms and the N has an extra but short leg that could have been considered an M rather than an N. But someone found these things in one of the other ships and thought it looked much like ZEANORIA. So, the aliens were named Zeanorians. I think it's interesting and could be humorous, too. Suppose this is only a brand name from their planet?"

"What does brand name mean?" Eric asked, frowning.

"Didn't you learn about that when you went to school? On earth there were large companies that manufactured things and the companies had names such as General Electric, Westinghouse, and Plymouth. There were thousands of such names. But it could be that the people who discovered the alien ships actually named the aliens after a manufacturing brand name." She laughed. "I guess it would be the same as calling humans General Electricians or Westinghousers. An alien race calling us that, I mean, if they found the names in one of our ships."

"You're really enthused about the ship, aren't you?"

"I'd almost forgotten. When I was just a teenager, my adopted grandfather, a Tech, gave me a report he'd written about one of the Zeanorian ships. He and some others studied a ship and the artifacts. I was fascinated. I wanted to be an archaeologist specializing in alien races. But, of course, that wasn't possible."

Eric had to coax her through the remainder of the ship. There were several unused compartments and one he had set aside as the bathroom.

Alicia was impressed when they reached the compartment reserved as the bedroom. There were comfortable blankets in one corner and a casual bed of sorts with pillows that Eric had traded a tiger skin for. Anticipating Alicia's arrival, he had put a small vase of flowers near the blanket—and a gift, a box of jewelry he had traded several tiger skins for.

"Where did you get all these?" Alicia asked incredulously, going through the collection of diamonds, emeralds, rubies and other stones.

She kissed him on the cheek lightly, but he turned her head and kissed her on the mouth, hard. Moments later he began caressing her body.

"Is that all you ever think of?" she said teasingly.

"Well, this is our honeymoon."

"We're so sweaty and grimy from the jungle. Why don't we take a bath first? Then we can relax and enjoy ourselves.

"Sounds like a good idea," Eric said, grinning, thinking of the pleasures of her body when freshly bathed, naked, and scented with exotic perfumes reserved especially for the women of the towers.

"You take your bath first," Alicia suggested. "I'll stay here awhile and admire your beautiful gifts."

Eric nodded agreement, pleased at the expression on her face as she kept on examining the diamonds, emeralds, and rubies. The gems were a thousand times more plentiful on Earth Two than they had been on earth and their value was additionally far less. But gems were still valued as gifts for women. He went to the bathroom and bathed hurriedly, congratulating himself on his thoughtfulness. The stones had impressed her and put her in a very loving mood.

Tying a towel around his waist, he hurried through the alien starship, returned to the bedroom to find—

Alicia had vanished.

He ran through the ship, searching every compartment until, at the doorway of the storage room, he saw her—

Sitting with her back towards him. She was intently studying one of the Zeanorian machines the size of a large stone. It was covered with buttons and levers of a dozen types. As Eric moved slowly into the room he realized with some astonishment that these artifacts from a dead race intrigued Alicia more than his gift of pretty baubles. She had been drawn back to this room and these alien remnants.

He sat nearby. She looked up, absently, deep in thought.

"These are fascinating," she said. "Did you ever have a dream you'd nearly forgotten? My dream of being an archaeologist was like that. I'd forgotten it for years until now . . . This thing, for example, well, I suppose it's crude to call it that. This machine, look at all the buttons and levers. So many types. Why? Each type must serve a distinct function. But what? And how? I think the Zeanorians are maddeningly interesting. Where did they come from? Which part of the universe and which galaxy? Were they taking part in an intergalactic war as we were? Or were they leaving a dying world? Could it be their ships were an experimental colony? Why did they land here? Was this choice of a planet simply an accident, or chosen for one reason or another?

"Why did they all die so rapidly? The experts who've examined their remains claim the ships landed here simultaneously and that all the Zeanorians died moments after landing. Was it an incredibly quick-acting disease or some sort of death weapon from one of their enemies?

"This machine, what does it do? Wouldn't you give your right arm to know?" She touched one of the buttons cautiously. Nothing happened.

"The buttons and levers are all marked in their language. See? It must take a certain sequence to make this machine do what it does, whatever that is. I know what I should do. I should write down the signs or codes or whatever it is on these controls. Make some kind of list. And be as systematic as I can.

She touched two levers in succession, biting her lower lip as she concentrated.

Eric had never seen Alicia so talkative, so enthused, so engrossed in a subject, or so unaware of him.

"Alicia . . ."

She turned to look at him with blank eyes.

"I finished my bath," he said lamely.

"Oh. I'll take mine now. Why don't you go to bed and rest awhile?" She winked suggestively.

"You may need your rest."

Eric grinned and went back to bed, stretched out, and closed his eyes.

He awoke hours later. He knew he'd slept hours because of the sensations throughout his body. Every muscle had that tone of relaxation that only hours of sleep could bring.

Alicia was not there.

Returning to the storage room, Eric was startled to see a group of savage aliens armed with spears.

15

"They won't touch us," Meyer bragged. "They're too well trained. Under extreme circumstances they might damage our trackers, but there's no chance of their killing or even hurting one of us."

"How do you mean too well trained?" Florence queried. She disliked Meyer. He was fat and arrogant and lazy. She had nothing against overweight people but hated arrogance and laziness. He had spoken of the Outsiders as if they were animals that had been trained.

"Exactly what I said," Meyer went on. "Too well trained. Trained by the way our society is constructed. Hurting one of us must be unthinkable to them. The Outsiders have no concept of revolution or war or resistance. We're the ones who said, 'This is a revolution.' The Outsiders didn't declare a revolution. They destroyed some of our trackers in an attempt to protect one of their members, that's all.''

Williamson, a mild-mannered Tech, cleared his throat and said, "When you say Outsiders, do you mean the Tree People and Herb-Seekers, or do you include all the outside tribes?''

Down at the edge of the river a small group of men were standing near the air cable and one of them suddenly shouted, "She's found it! She gave the signal!''

Meyer seemed not to notice. He answered Williamson, "When I say Outsiders, I mean all the tribes—Tree People, Herb-Seekers, Hunters, Archers, Fishermen, whatever. They were trained from birth, at Homebase until puberty, and then by the adults of whatever tribe they were shipped off to. There's another factor, too. Everyone knows the most intelligent have always been kept at Homebase.''

Florence seethed inwardly. It was true that I.Q. tests were given to all the children and that, as a general rule, the most intelligent were kept at Homebase to become Techs or Guiders or Researchers or Historians, but it was not all a matter of I.Q. If a child showed a high mechanical ability along with his high I.Q., he was usually kept at Homebase to become a Tech. On the other hand, there were often children with equally high I.Q.'s who demonstrated great physical prowess and these were sent to the Outsiders. The concept that everyone at Homebase was smarter than everyone outside was a popular myth that she resented since it reeked of bigotry.

It seemed to Florence that most members of their

little scouting party were not taking the mission seriously. Eight men and two women. Only four trackers controlled by portable consoles.

We're in the middle of what our ancestors would have called enemy territory and there isn't a single person on guard, she thought.

Everyone was watching Joan as she emerged from the water with X-20 in her arms. Some of the men cheered and Joan took off her air helmet. Walking with an exaggerated sway of hips, all eyes were turned in her direction, and Florence knew all those eyes were not focused on the furry body of X-20. Judging by the expression on the men's faces, most of them were staring at Joan's lush body. It was said that she was the sexiest woman at Homebase and rumored that she had turned down President Bromfield repeatedly because she did not like him, making love with almost every other man at Homebase simply to frustrate him.

Joan set the mechanical animal on the ground and knelt beside it. She leaned, supposedly to examine the tracker, but Florence felt she might be doing it because it caused her lush breasts to strain against the scanty swimsuit. She was sexy, all right, Florence admitted, and she was giving off torrid emanations. Even as a woman she could sense it and see the effects on the men. Joan was egotistical, Florence knew, and if possible she would make love with all eight men tonight, that is, if some of them didn't mind waiting.

"This is impossible," Hastings muttered as he knelt bside X-20. "Something cut through the metal."

Purnell examined the tracker also, shoulder to shoulder with Hastings. "It happened," Purnell said. "The Tree People have something that can cut through metal. That means they can stop any of our trackers." He looked up with something akin to fear in his expression and then looked down at the arrow in his chest that had appeared there abruptly as if part of a magician's act. Blood bubbled around the shaft.

Hastings had turned toward Purnell and an arrow appeared silently in his throat. The turn became a synchronized part of the downward motion as he toppled, as if a choreographer had neatly included this movement of death into the dance of life.

Florence heard a hiss of air and saw a blur of movement from the corner of an eye. An arrow thunked into Meyer's chest, while another almost simultaneously struck his back squarely between the shoulder blades. Florence saw all the men die quickly, almost silently. Eight men chopped down before they could raise a hand in defense. If President Bromfield and the others knew . . .

She rose, her heartbeat beginning to quicken as she waited for an arrow to end her life. Joan was standing also, waiting.

The Archers left the cover of trees and bushes. She counted rapidly. Forty. They had been outnumbered four to one without even knowing it. Now, since only Joan and she were left alive, they were outnumbered twenty to one.

As the men came nearer, Florence saw the expressions on their faces and knew the Archers had no intention of killing Joan and her.

16

The aliens were humanoid in height, shape, and general size, but with green skin, bulbous eyes, and antennae that protruded from the tops of their heads. Their teeth were like fangs and their six digit hands appeared wide and strong.

Alicia was still sitting in the same position.

The aliens raised their spears to hurl at Alicia.

She saw Eric from the corner of an eye at the same time that he realized the aliens were not three dimensional. They were a flickering image on the compartment wall, an incredibly realistic image.

"I activated it," Alicia said, looking at Eric from the corners of her eyes, unable to divert her full attention. "It happened by accident, but it happened! This is a projector like the old film projectors with a built in microstorage of the information units. This particular film or unit seems to be a history of the Zeanorian race."

Alicia's voice dwindled away to silence as the primitive aliens were shown attacking a large creature much like a dinosaur. Eric was interested in their tactics and their use of spears. He sat and watched with great interest for awhile, but then as the projector went on to show the Zeanorians building their first cities, the roots of their civilization, his interest decreased steadily. When he began falling asleep while watching the film, he gave up and went back to the bedroom. The next morning Alicia was there beside him. She said the projector had stopped of its own accord only a few minutes ago and she did not want to start it again since it apparently operated seven or eight hours continuously once activated. Alicia was so exhausted that she fell asleep.

It was late in the day when they resumed their journey. Eric was slashing through the jungle with a mechanical sweep of the sword, changing it from hand to hand occasionally and favoring his injured shoulder when, suddenly, the dense growth ended.

They came upon an area where all the vegetation had been trampled flat. They were able to walk comfortably and Eric led the way, wondering what had caused this strange section. They were near the Valley of Tigers now and he had not seen anything like this before. Strange, he thought, because he had covered this area many times.

All the growth except the thickest of trees had been torn down. The ground was covered with a mat of dead and decaying vegetation mingled with grasslike growths that still lived. It was like walking on a thick, springy carpet and Eric remembered he had seen something like this years before.

As the memory clicked in his mind, Alicia screamed. He heard a crunching sound and whirled around to see Alicia sliding into a hole at least four feet in diameter. He dropped the sword and grabbed one of her wrists an instant before she disappeared from sight.

While he helped Alicia to stand erect, a series of sounds came from the opening. A sliding, whispery sound of movement. A sound of life and breathing unlike any Eric had ever heard before.

A python emerged from the hole, its obsidian eyes gleaming darkly in the sunlight. For a moment Eric was paralyzed by the sight of the slithering body, so long and scaled, so unlike anything else he had ever seen. He grabbed his sword but at that moment he saw Alicia stumble and fall. The python's tongue darted to strike Alicia's shoulder. She rose to her feet once more, walked a few yards and collapsed. Eric remembered the stories, the fantastic stories that he had heard and hardly believed.

Some of the Hunters had said that pythons could strike a creature as large as a tiger or a man and that the poison from its tongue paralyzed its victim. One Hunter claimed he had seen a tiger struck and remain motionless, powerless while the huge snake-like creature swallowed it whole.

Once, years ago, Eric had seen an area like this and the Hunter with him had said it appeared to be a nesting ground of pythons. For some reason, perhaps the very basic one of finding a better hunting ground, this python had moved to this area.

But even as these thoughts whirled through his

124

mind, Eric slashed at the creature's head. The tongue flickered in his direction. He slashed again and again until blood began to ooze through the thick skin.

Something burned the small of his back. He turned and saw another python. It had struck him from behind while he struggled to save Alicia. He had been stupid to assume that there was only one of the creatures to fight. He struck out at this new enemy, but even while the blade of the sword flashed through the air, he felt his muscles tighten with a strange paralysis. The Sword struck with a harmless, glancing blow.

His legs became powerless and he sank to his knees. He could see and think, but every muscle in his body was absolutely useless. He watched in horror as the wounded python opened his jaws and slithered toward Alicia as she lay helpless on the ground.

All the stories were true. The pythons were cold-blooded and did not feel pain. He had seriously wounded the first python, and it might bleed to death from the cut in its head, but first it would swallow Alicia.

17

Florence remained passive as she was blindfolded and tied at her wrists and ankles. She felt herself being placed into a canvas stretcherlike device, then carried away without a single word.

They are certainly organized! she thought. Eight men killed before they could make the slightest move in self-defense. And now Joan and herself being carried off, bound, blindfolded, with no confusion, no delay.

The trip lasted hours. There were times when she felt the brush of leaves and branches as they passed through thick growth. Once she heard the sound of a waterfall. The men spoke to each other occasionally, but no one spoke to her.

Finally she was seated in a chair, her wrists and ankles untied momentarily only to be retied to the chair. Last of all they removed the blindfold. She saw she was inside a large tent. She remembered hearing that the Archers were the only tribe of Outsiders who used tents. However, since they were nomadic there was no way of knowing where they were.

Someone removed the blindfold. Standing before her with his arms folded across his chest was a man she judged to be in his middle forties. There were flecks of gray in his hair at the temples. His arms were tanned and muscular. Rather handsome, she thought, with his squarish jaw and cool gray eyes.

"My name is Karl Springer," the man said evenly. "I am a colonel in the Archer Army and have the unpleasant task of informing you that you are our prisoner. We wish to have the answers to some questions."

"What sort of questions?"

"Let's start with an easy one. What's your name?" With a nod of his head he signaled the man standing behind her to leave the tent.

"My name is Florence Franklin," she said. "And if you want me to talk, I'll talk. I love to talk. What do you want to know? My past, present, future? My hobbies, my likes, dislikes? I like to do oil painting. I like flowers, music, pretty clothes, swimming, good food. I have to be careful about my fondness for food and watch my weight. So far I have a nice figure but I could easily gain too much weight and lose it all. At Homebase I have a position of what they call communications specialist. My tasks are varied. I do some writing—reports and so forth. Do you want me to talk about my friends? I can talk about the men and women I've known."

As she went on, Karl moved a chair before her's and sat, waiting, listening. Finally he said, "Shut up."

"That's not very polite."

"You have a big, smart mouth, don't you?"

"Sticks and stones will break my bones, but names will never hurt me." She managed to put a mocking tone into her voice but even as she did, something clicked in the back of her mind. Big, smart mouth, he'd said. And he was right, absolutely right. She'd always been mouthy and had sometimes said the wrong thing at the wrong time to the wrong person. She remembered in a flash that she'd fallen into President Bromfield's disfavor by openly criticizing him. Joan had also antagonized Bromfield. Likewise with Hastings. Meyer was a lazy bore. She flicked mentally through the names of the ten people who'd been on the scouting party and realized that Bromfield had disliked each for one reason or another.

And Bromfield selected those who went on the scouting party! Did he select us because he strongly suspected we'd all be killed? She wondered.

"We can try the sticks and stones bit and break some of your bones," the Archer said, and added quickly, "When is Homebase going to launch its next scouting party?"

"I don't have the slightest idea."

"What type of defenses are they installing at Homebase?"

"They didn't tell me and I can't guess."

"Is Homebase preparing any special types of weapons to combat the Outsiders?"

"None that I know of."

"What do you know?" Karl asked.

"Nothing."

"I'll see you again in a few minutes." As soon as the Archer named Karl left the room, three other men came into the tent. They cut the clothes away from her body, then untied her wrists and ankles. With a man holding each arm, they dragged her out of the tent and across an open area to a large wooden target. While she was still in a standing position, her ankles and wrists were once more tied, securing her in an awkward spread-eagled stance. A dozen or so men stood near the target, openly staring at her nude body.

Colonel Springer appeared in the crowd and watched for awhile as one of the Archers moved to a position some dozens of feet away. He went to stand beside Florence and said, "Searle is our best Archer. We're going to play a game. It's called 'letting Searle test his accuracy at greater and greater distances.' Keep your eyes open and you'll see how the game is played."

Florence felt humiliated to be nude before the eyes of so many men. Yet she told herself she would not show her true feelings, and gritted her teeth in an effort to keep her face expressionless.

The Archer named Searle shot an arrow into the target an inch from her shoulder. He took some paces further away and the next arrow landed half an inch from her hip.

"I don't quite understand this game," Florence said.

"You will in a minute." Searle moved further

from his human target and the next arrow nicked Florence's left arm as it thunked into the wood. "See?" Karl queried. "The further away Searle moves, the harder it is for him to hit close to you without actually hurting you." She could feel blood trickling down her arm. "He doesn't want to hurt you badly but he might do so unless you tell us what we want to hear. If you give the right answers, we'll let you down from the target."

Florence felt overwhelmingly outraged, her eyes widening with indignation. She curled a lip and sneered, "Aren't you the big colonel in the big army, playing dumb little boy games, tying poor, defenseless girls to targets and shooting at them? You bastard! You dirty bastard!"

Searle moved and shot another arrow which landed thunk in the meaty section of her left thigh. Florence's eyes filled with tears. She couldn't stop them. She bit her lower lip. The next arrow missed her body but the one after that struck her arm, pinning it to the wooden target.

"Oh, stop it, please," she moaned. "Please, please, please."

"We can't stop until you've given the right answers," Colonel Springer said coldly. "And you must realize, Searle is moving so far away that he can no longer guarantee where the arrows will strike. He does his best to come close and not hit you but it's entirely possible that an arrow might take off an ear or a finger. He'll soon be so far away that an arrow might strike your heart and end the whole game altogether."

"I'll talk," she said abruptly. "Take me back to

the tent. Please. I'll tell you everything you want to know.''

They removed the arrows from her body and untied her wrists and ankles. One of the men helped her limp back to the tent. Once more she was tied to the chair.

"Talk," Colonel Springer urged.

Florence chewed her lower lip and fought the impulse of fresh tears. The bastards weren't bandaging her wounds. They were still oozing blood, fresh red blood, *her* blood dribbling down onto the ground.

"Why don't you stop the bleeding before I bleed to death?" she questioned.

Colonel Springer glanced at the bloody holes in her otherwise flawless body. "Talk first and then we'll patch you up."

"Well, the truth is I don't know anything that would be of value to you. There was a conference about the revolution. I attended it and they made a decision to send out a scouting party to recover the experimental tracker. That's all I know. Honest.''

Karl Springer studied her long moments and then said, "I think you know more than that."

"That's all," she affirmed.

He left the tent and returned in a short time with two other men. One carried a brazier with burning coals and the other carried a branding iron.

"Our next step is to employ a method used by our ancestors," Springer said. "It's called torture." He chuckled briefly but without humor.

"Torture?" she replied blankly.

"There are many kinds of torture," Springer

said, "but the kind we find most effective is the branding iron. I'll tell you how it works. We'll start by branding your breasts. The scars will be permanent. If you haven't talked by the time we've burned each breast a dozen times, we'll start on your pretty face. We can turn your face into something that no man would want to look at."

"You're joking," she said lightly. "You don't want information that badly, do you?"

"Please believe me," Springer said earnestly. "This is a matter of life and death. If Homebase is planning other steps such as this first scouting party, I want to know. And I have to know about their defenses because we will plan attacks." He leaned closer until their faces were only inches apart. She could see tiny beads of perspiration on his upper lip. For the first time she noticed the silver insignia of an eagle that denoted the rank of colonel, one on each shoulder. "The lives of my brothers and friends hang in the balance," Springer said.

He waited for her response but she remained silent.

"This is your last chance. We want the answers to three basic questions. When is Homebase going to launch its next scouting party? What kinds of defenses already exist or are planning to be installed? What sort of weaponry have they prepared or have started to prepare?"

"I don't know any answers to those questions," she snapped. "You bastards! How could you possibly have the incredible nerve to torture me!"

Springer could see the disbelief in her face and

eyes. He sighed. "All right, we'll convince you we're not bluffing. Ellin." Springer touched her left breast with his forefinger. "Make the first mark right here. It's a tender area that will be partially hidden by her arm, and if she doesn't talk after the first brand, work your way toward the front of the breast."

Florence licked her lips and her entire body tensed. "You can't—"

But the red hot branding iron was placed against her flesh and the pain roared up to her skull.

She screamed and fainted.

When she slowly regained consciousness, the first image she saw was one of the Colonel's eagle emblems. A spot of sunlight gleamed on the metal, causing it to glitter. Springer and the other men did not notice or did not care. They were all staring at her. She felt a wave of vertigo, a sensation of unreality. She was sweaty, breathing raggedly, and her thoughts were confused. She saw a thin shaft of sunlight from a tiny hole in the tent ceiling. It was what caused the spot of light that glittered on the Colonel's silver eagle. Beautiful in a way, she thought.

"Did that convince you I don't know anything?" she mumbled weakly.

"No, not really."

"You bastards," she murmured. "You dirty, filthy bastards."

"We're not dirty or filthy," Springer said. "All of us took a shower this morning and we'll let you take a shower, too. If you just give us the answers we want."

133

"Go to hell," Florence spat.

"Then we'll make another mark in your pretty, precious flesh," Springer said.

"How can you do this to me?"

The ugly man named Ellin was about to reach for the branding iron when Florence heard a distant scream.

"Who was that?" she gasped.

"Your companion."

"Joan?" The scream came again, this time longer and more shrill, ending abruptly as if Joan had fainted at a peak of agony. "What are they doing to her?"

Springer said bitterly, "You'll find out when we start doing the same thing to you if you don't answer our questions. I wish you would talk, Florence. I hate to see you suffer so much."

"Fine friend," Florence quipped. "With friends like you, I don't need enemies."

"Make the next mark, Ellin. Close to the first."

Florence held her breath as the ugly man brought the branding iron so close to her breast that she could feel the heat despite the pulsating pain of the first brand.

"Want to talk?" Springer questioned.

"Go screw yourself," Florence hissed, her eyes glaring.

Colonel Springer sighed. The man named Ellin did not touch her with the branding iron. Instead he replaced it on the brazier.

"You were bluffing?" Florence said. "You only planned to make one brand to see if you could break me down?"

"That's right."

"You're giving up?"

"No. We have something more effective than a branding iron. Something guaranteed to make you talk. It could make a brass monkey talk. I didn't want to use it but I see now we'll have to. There wouldn't be any point in disfiguring your body and burning it repeatedly. Our next step is even more painful and it doesn't destroy the flesh."

"More painful?" Florence repeated faintly.

The man named Ellin was studying her nude body with great interest, the expression on his face unmistakable. He turned toward Springer and said respectfully, "Colonel, why don't we take a break and take her before we use that gadget? She'll be in bad shape afterwards, not much fun."

For some reason Florence felt more horrified by this proposal than she had by the torture. At least the pain had been a human element in its own way. But the bastard named Ellin had suggested they use her like an inanimate object, a thing with no identity, a nonhuman!

"Let's finish the questioning first," Springer said. He left the tent and returned in what seemed half a minute with a strange looking device in his right hand. "You've heard of the Zeanorian spaceships?"

"Certainly," Florence snarled irritably. "Everyone on Earth Two knows about the alien starships."

"This is one of the devices found on a Zeanorian ship. It has its own power source and emits a blue ray. I don't know what the aliens used it for. Perhaps they used it to brush their teeth or scratch their backs, but it has a strange effect on the human nervous system. We call it the Zeanorian persuader because it is the equivalent of a whip or torture rack or any other ancient device. The control mechanism can give a variable strength depending upon what's needed and Ellin knows how to use this as well as the branding iron.''

Springer handed the alien egg-shaped object to the other man and Ellin held it by the handlelike stem, aiming the device at the lower portion of her naked body.

The blue ray bathed her flesh and gave the sensation of being burned by a huge flame. She knew immediately that this was their last trick and knew also that it would succeed, would make her talk and betray everyone in Homebase. The human body could only endure so much pain and then the brain began to give its welfare primary importance.

Colonel Springer said, ''I would suggest you talk before the persuader ruins your nervous system.''

She kept enduring the pain somehow. She heard a faint hum from the alien machine. Taking a deep breath, she was about to say she would tell them anything they wanted to know but couldn't. She began to scream. And scream. And scream.

The screaming stopped.

18

Eric felt half dead when he saw the dark-haired angel drift from the sky. He had always thought Alicia the most beautiful woman in the world, but now this woman seemed even more attractive and fascinating in mysterious ways that he could not understand.

Her long, dark hair flowed around the curves of her naked shoulders. She was large-breasted, slender-waisted, and long-legged. She wore a two-piece suit of a blue material that appeared to be metallic and which glimmered faintly in the sunlight. The bottom part fitted tightly across her hips, low and as scanty as Alicia's undergarments. The halter was little more than a strip of cloth that cupped her breasts to cover the nipples. She wore a pair of shoes that were made of a blue cloth similar to the other garments but much more firm. And on each ankle of the shoes a small, white wing.

Eric was reminded of all the fables he had heard during his boyhood, stories of a race of mermaids that lived in the sea, of naked women who lived in caves in the mountains, and legends of a race of women that lived on a mesa beyond the mountains, women who wore wings on their ankles and could fly through the air. As a boy he had believed the stories as most boys did. As a man he had scoffed at the tales, following the inclination of the other Hunters who scoffed and called the stories fairy tales for children, dismissing them as having no basis in fact.

But here was one of the angels dropping from the sky.

She wore a thick belt with strange instruments. Dangling from the belt on one side was an attachment that Eric recognized from sketches of how life had been on earth many centuries ago, a contrivance called a gun holster.

And she also carried a ruby knife identical to the one the Tree Father had given him.

The Tree Father had said, I know of only one other knife such as this one.

Who owns the other knife? Eric had asked.

I will tell you someday. Return with your Alicia. I would like to meet her, and perhaps I will tell you then.

Last of all Eric noticed the gun in the woman's hands. She aimed it at the python. The snake whirled its huge head upward, its poisonous tongue flickering near the woman's legs.

Its head disappeared!

Eric felt consciousness fading, and as it faded, he

stared in disbelief at the long reptilian body that writhed headless, writhed reflexively, blindly.

The woman turned to fire at the python that had struck him from behind, and then Eric sank into a sparkling darkness. He knew this black spell was caused by the reptile's venom and wondered if Alicia and he would die from the poison.

Somewhere in the deep darkness he experienced an oasis of a dream. The dark-haired angel was carrying Alicia and himself far above the ground. Alicia and he were magically weightless and the angel towed them through the air with lengths of rope tied to their waists. For one brief interval the angel in the dream was close enough that he could feel her long dark hair tickling his cheek, and once he felt the ripeness of her breasts brush his shoulder. They passed through the billowy white walls of a cloud canyon. This is a fantastic dream, he thought.

But the sensation of the woman's hair and flesh had been as real as the touch of Alicia's, as real as anything he had ever experienced in his whole life.

19

When Florence regained consciousness, she saw that, as Colonel Springer had stated, her body had not been damaged—at least not outwardly. But the effect on her nervous system, however, had been tremendous. Every nerve in her body was still tingling from the strange ray.

"Let's try that again," she said defiantly. A plan formed in her mind. Each fainting spell was a release from the agony. Could she use those periods of unconsciousness as an oasis to help endure the torturing until they tired of this game and gave up?

Ellin used the alien instrument over and over until she fainted each time. He methodically revived her with a splash of cold water and other methods, forcing her up from the comfort of unconsciousness. She felt her mind start to slip and reach a bleak plateau during which nothing seemed real. She saw Colonel Springer standing behind Ellin, faint tears in Springer's eyes as if he totally regretted the course they had embarked upon.

And, finally, gasping for breath, she said, "I don't know anything about future scouting parties or defenses or new weaponry, but maybe I can help you some other way. President Bromfield will be making most of the decisions during the revolution. I can tell you everything I know about him, his habits, his past life, the decisions he's made, his personality, his way of thinking. All that should help you anticipate his moves."

"That could be very useful," Colonel Springer agreed.

She started telling them about Bromfield, and another of the Archers was called in to witness. She talked for what seemed hours. At her request they untied her wrists and ankles. She talked again, and they gave her something to eat; more information, and she requested clothing. They gave her a short green robe to wear.

She found she could not stop trembling. Her hands trembled so badly she had difficulty holding a glass of water without spilling it.

"That's enough for today," Colonel Springer said. He nodded and the other men left the tent.

Florence's shoulders slumped slightly. She felt totally defeated. She did not want her captors to know this and decided to keep up a front somehow.

"You bastards are really thorough, aren't you?"

Colonel Springer did not answer the question. He moved a chair beside her's and said, "Here's a salve for the burned area. It'll stop most of the pain." He held a jar, dipped his fingers into the whitish sub-

141

stance and gently spread it on the damaged area of her breast. It soothed the aching sensation of the burn and then he applied a bandage to contain the salve.

"What happens now?" Florence asked.

"Guess."

"I'm placed in solitary confinement until the next session?"

He nodded negatively.

"I'll be placed in a cell with Joan so we'll be able to chit-chat?"

"Not today."

"I'm going to be raped."

Springer nodded affirmatively.

"By the whole Archer army?" Florence said, feeling her eyes widen at the thought.

"Possibly."

"How do you mean possibly?"

"It has been suggested by my aides that I choose either your friend or yourself as my personal and exclusive mate, and that the other woman be given to the officers for their pleasure."

"How many officers are there?"

"Twenty."

He was very handsome, she thought. And his fingers had been gentle when he applied the salve to her breast. There was something nice in his eyes. He had supervised the questioning and torture, but acted as if he did it with the greatest of reluctance, and only because it had been absolutely necessary. She remembered the trace of tears in his eyes during the torturing. The man named Ellin on the other hand had been a sadistic monster, obviously enjoying watching her squirm in agony. Colonel Springer was tall and strong, obviously intelligent and competent, a dedicated leader. He was the most handsome and appealing man she had ever met.

So she said, "Why don't you choose Joan? She's prettier and sexier and better in bed."

"Let me be the judge of that," Colonel Springer said with a faint smile.

"I'll put it another way," Florence said. "I think you're a filthy bastard and I think I'll throw up if you touch me. I don't want you. I'd rather make love with a snake. I volunteer to be the pet of the twenty officers."

20

There were periods during the following days that seemed like dreams and other periods that felt like nightmares. He regained consciousness in a small room with featureless stone walls as if they had been carved from solid rock. His body was filled with pain almost constantly in the beginning. At times the pain was so great he could hardly resist the impulse to cry out in agony. Sleep at first came only when he lost consciousness from complete exhaustion. He was informed that the python venom would be fatal unless treated properly. After days of agony, he sometimes wished it had been. The paralysis, however, gradually subsided and the pain slowly diminished. He was informed that Alicia was in another room, recovering nicely, but it would be wise not to see each other again until they were both more fully recovered.

He learned their rescuer was named Vita. She visited him daily and fed him facts and scraps of information as his health improved and as he was able to comprehend.

She said she was a member of a subcolony that had been originated centuries ago with the mission of making the Zeanorian starships operable. Their existence was kept secret from the members of Homebase and the tribes such as the Hunters and Tree People.

At this point in the explanation, Eric was lucid enough to ask, "Why keep your efforts secret from everyone?"

"It was decided that we could work more effectively if we were self-supporting, self-governing, free from outside influences and controls. Still, with the least amount of restrictions, it has taken centuries to study the alien starships and reach the point where we think we may be able to make one of the ships operable within the next year."

Eric learned that the subcolony assigned to the study of the alien starships had deliberately started and maintained the rumors about mermaids and cavewomen.

"Our grandparents started this mission," Vita explained. "Those in control of Homebase at the time reported the subcolony as destroyed after a few months. All contacts with Homebase were cut off and we became fully self-supporting." Vita smiled faintly. "When I say all contacts, I mean all contacts of a generally known nature. We have three agents in Homebase who keep us informed of matters there. And we have agents in each of the tribes—the Hunters, Tree People, Archers . . ."

"Spies?"

Vita laughed. "We do not consider them as dramatic as spies. We prefer to think of them as anonymous contacts."

"Who is your contact with the Hunters?"

"I'd rather not tell you because it would be bad policy to tell such information when there is no need. But I will tell you our contact with the Tree People."

"Who?"

"You may be able to guess the truth. It concerns the knife you lost in the river."

"The Tree Father's ruby knife?"

"Yes."

"You have an identical knife."

"Yes, I do."

"Mine must be magical," Eric admitted. "It can cut through metal. No ordinary knife can do that. And it returned to its sheath on my belt."

"The cutting through metal is not magic," Vita said. "The Tree Father explained to you that it cut metal because of molecular vibration. They are Zeanorian tools used to work with metal. We have never been able to take one apart to study the power source, but there is a constant regeneration of energy that has a side effect like that of a radio beam. When you carried the knife I was able to follow you through the jungle by means of a—the old word on Earth was radar, I believe. But one of our technicians here developed a type of sensor that could detect the energy signal from the knife, and—"

Something had clicked in Eric's mind. He said, "The Tree Father said he knew of only one other knife such as the one he gave me. You carry the second knife. He said to keep the knife with me always. So—"

"You have seen the truth," Vita confirmed. "The Tree Father is one of our agents."

21

"You don't have any choice in the matter," Colonel Springer said grimly. "Can you walk? My quarters are in the adjoining tent, through that flap."

Florence rose, walked two yards on wobbly legs, and collapsed. As she rolled over on her back Karl knelt by her side.

"I think I'm going to live," she said, "but my legs don't feel too good."

He picked her up and carried her into the other tent, placing her gently on a mat in a corner. "Why don't you rest awhile and take a shower?"

"You want me to clean up before you sample me?" she retorted. "Hell. Take your sample this way while I'm still dirty and sweaty and half dead."

Colonel Karl Springer lowered his eyes and she saw a bit of the shy boy in him. She remembered her first shy lovers. He said, "I thought you might want to shower first. I have some perfume you could use and a nightgown . . ."

She glanced to one side, following his gaze, and saw a filmy blue nightgown spread across a cushion nearby.

"What kind of beast are you?" she growled. "Are you out of your mind? You tear me apart to get information, and then you want me to bathe and slip in a sexy nightgown and put on perfume so you can shift into a romantic role and make love to me like some sort of conquering hero? Bullshit." Still lying flat on her back, she quickly unbuttoned the green robe, separated it to expose her body once more, and simultaneously spread her legs. "Let's get it over with," she said.

She closed her eyes. She could hear the whisper of his clothing as he undressed. A moment later he was on top of her. She could feel him trembling faintly with what she knew must be his mixture of anticipation and anxiousness. She almost cried out with pleasure when he entered her, it felt so good. Somehow she managed to remain quiet. He was very passionate and climaxed quickly. He remained joined and began kissing her forehead and cheeks, whispering, "You're so beautiful, so very beautiful."

"I'll bet you tell that to every girl you rape," she quipped.

"And so courageous."

"I was frightened silly the whole time," she contradicted.

He began kissing her on the mouth and she felt him become fully aroused again. He made love to her again and climaxed a second time.

149

"I want you," he whispered when he finished. "I want you forever and ever." Once more he fondled and caressed her.

"You must be out of your mind," she retorted. "Joan is sexier and prettier."

"I want you," he insisted.

When he moved above her, she made a face and said, "Again?" and closed her eyes. After he climaxed a third time, she said, "Is it all over? I think I'll take a shower now. Where is it?"

"Through that flap over there. You'll find towels, washclothes, soap."

As Florence crossed the tent, she saw alien devices that resembled the Zeanorian torture appliance, but ones that apparently served other purposes. She wondered if she could coax Karl into explaining the function of each. She decided it would not be a difficult task to manipulate him, and she knew the weeks or months ahead could well be the most exciting and interesting in her whole life.

She went into the shower stall and closed the flap behind her, discovering the cubicle had been formed with wooden sides and a wooden flooring. The walls were tightly edge to edge but the floorboards were about half an inch apart to allow a drain for the water. Directly beneath the shower head was a small rubber mat. Slipping out of the green robe, turning on the water, and reaching for a cake of soap, Florence felt her knees give way completely. She fell with a loud thud. The questioning had exhausted her and, although she had been careful to hide her response from Karl, she had experienced multiple orgasms during his lovemaking. The

150

two combined had been too much, and she felt as weak as a baby.

"Are you all right?" Karl called after hearing a thud.

Florence sat with her back against one of the wooden walls, a dreamy smile on her face as the water sprayed her nude body. She began to half-heartedly soap herself. She replied happily, "I dropped the soap, that's all."

22

For long moments Eric was silent, staring at Vita. It seemed incredible that the Tree Father and Vita knew each other.

"The Tree Father and I have been in contact with each other for many years," Vita explained. "And the revolution has been brewing for quite awhile. When the Father learned you planned to kidnap Alicia, he decided it could be the spark for the revolution. The Guiders and Techs were certain to pursue you—and kill you if possible. It was decided to use the Archers to protect you against pursuers. My function was to stay aware of your location and keep the Archers informed. Everything went well until you lost the Tree Father's knife in the river. I had to dive underwater three times before I managed to locate it with the help of the sensor."

"So you found the knife. But how did it—"

Vita drew the weapon strapped around her waist

and showed Eric the control knobs. "One person could rule a nation of savages with this Zeanorian weapon. It can discharge a disintegrator ray. And it can kill or only stun."

"Stun?"

"Yes, by a setting on this knob." She pointed at the knob. "And it can stun the nervous system of any man or animal."

Vita went on to explain that after she had recovered the knife from the river, she couldn't locate Eric and Alicia in the maze of jungle.

"I knew you would be moving on toward the Valley of Tigers, but I didn't know where you were beneath that layer of jungle. I had two choices. Keep trying to find you or go on to the Valley and wait for you there. I didn't want to give up. I estimated your location and rate of travel. After trying to locate you visually with no luck, I began coming down into the tree tops of the jungle. I'd sit absolutely still for several minutes and listen. After several times I heard you hacking through the jungle with Colonel Springer's sword. Then I was able to stay informed of your location but it was difficult crouching in tree tops, sweating, listening, sweating, listening until my ears ached and then moving on to another tree.

"After awhile I realized you were headed toward the nearest sundra. I took a chance, went there, and waited. When you and Alicia appeared, I used the Zeanorian gun and stunned both of you. I replaced the Tree Father's knife in its sheath while you and Alicia were unconscious. When you started moving again the next day, it was again easy to keep track of

153

your location." Eric saw she was watching his reactions very carefully at this point. "Because of the Zeanorian antigravity belt, I was able to float with the breeze at times. It's like floating on a cloud. I want to—later—show you how it can be done."

But Eric was confused by many things, too confused to fully understand the invitation or to notice the expression on Vita's face.

"There are three or four things I don't understand," he said. "It may be unimportant, but earlier you said the subcolony deliberately started false rumors about mermaids and cavewomen. Why? What purpose did that serve?"

Camouflage," Vita answered. "We call ourselves the Zeanorian Angels for several reasons. Although we are descendants of a race and civilization entirely different than the Zeanorians, we have been studying them for centuries. We've salvaged every one of their antigravity belts and are now able to fly as high as the clouds. We lead a life of scientific research isolated from the rest of our society on this planet. The subcolony started the rumors of unbelievable mermaids and cavewomen so that when someone heard an occasional rumor of a woman flying through the air, they would automatically disregard it as one of the fables. You see, we, the Angels, are included psychologically in the same group as the mermaids and cavewomen. Occasionally one of us is spotted in the sky. But the person is simply not believed. No more than he would be believed if he said he saw a mermaid. The wings on our shoes are a little theatrical but they were deliberately started by our ancestors. The wings are supposed to

154

be magical, to play on the superstitions and uneducated imaginings of the tribes."

Eric did not fully understand but he could grasp some of the logic.

"You said you are able to fly because of Zeanorian antigravity belts?"

"Yes."

"How do they work?"

Vita smiled at the question. "It would take me days to explain only the fundamental concepts. My mother spent half her lifetime studying the technology behind the machinery and methods they used to overcome gravity."

As Eric slowly recovered, he wanted to see Alicia. His requests were denied.

A short, dark-haired woman named Sheila had been assigned to him as his nurse. She brought him his meals and medication, bathed him when the paralysis was too great for him to do so alone, and helped him as he regained greater and greater use of his arms and hands. He soon saw that she was interested in him. She went to great lengths to conceal her interest when others were around but began letting Eric know how she felt.

One night Sheila brought him a late meal and explained to him how the subcolony had established itself in the depths of a mesa surrounded by vast stretches of desert. The caves had been carved by Zeanorian disintegrator guns, Sheila explained. The subcolony founders had wanted to make their base as inaccessible as possible, one surrounded by a desert that individuals or tribes would find impossible to cross with their limited means, and one atop a mesa that would be impossible to climb.

"Our ancestors named our base the Aerie," Sheila said, "a more colorful word for nest. And this base is like an eagle's nest." She was breathing deeply, studying him as she sat close. "How do you feel tonight?"

"Much better," Eric replied.

Sheila toyed with the hem of her skirt as it lay across her thighs. Eric watched as she raised the garment to her waist to show she wore nothing beneath. She said in a near whisper, "Are you recovered enough?"

It was Eric's turn to take a deep breath as he responded to the vision of the dark thatch between Sheila's thighs.

He groaned.

Sheila smiled as she moved closer. "I think you may need something other than food."

She was touching him with her fingertips, loosening his clothing, and reaching inside to grasp him. Her voice grew soft but husky as she moved against him. "Let's give our bodies what they need. Let's forget everything else and enjoy ourselves."

Eric was tumbled into a sexual world he had never known. Alicia had been gentle and loving, passive, satisfying in those ways; Sheila was aggressive, demanding, wild. She bit his shoulder. She clawed his back. She was constantly in motion, moving beneath him, arching her lithe body against him, moaning, and sometimes whispering for him to go harder or faster. She drained him and came back the next night.

23

When Karl returned from the first raid on Home-base, Florence tried to appear casual. She prepared a simple meal. They ate alone in his tent. Her hands had been trembling from the effects of the Zeanorian persuader. It was humiliating to sit there with him and have her hands tremble as she held a cup or glass, humiliating because it gave the appearance of fear. I'm not afraid, she thought rebelliously, not frightened of him or anything else!

"How did the attack go?" she inquired as casually as possible.

"I think it would be best if I didn't tell you too many details, for your own peace of mind and welfare."

They ate in silence awhile, sitting on opposite sides of the small table.

"Why?" she said sarcastically. "Do you think I could escape? And return to Homebase with vital information? I went outside today. These tent walls are driving me crazy. I wanted to get a breath of fresh air, see something different. You said I could leave anytime I wanted. Leave and walk around the—What did you call it?''

"Compound."

"You said I could walk around the compound. But there are guards everywhere. They kept saying, 'Sorry, you can't go beyond this point.' 'Sorry, this area is off limits.' There are dozens of guards out there! Do you really think you need so many to keep me from escaping?''

Karl smiled faintly. "You flatter yourself. Those guards are out there for security reasons, to keep a Guider or Tech from infiltrating our compound. They have incidentally been told to keep you out of certain areas.''

"And one of your little tin soldiers followed me everywhere I went," Florence complained. "He kept at a distance, but he made certain I was always in his sight.''

"He was instructed to be certain you were not harmed in any way.''

"I saw Joan today," Florence went on. "She's as happy as a lark. She has twenty men. They're treating her like a queen. She gets plenty of sex and anything else she wants. I have only one man. You!''

The dig hurt his pride. Her lips began to tug with a smile of satisfaction. To hide the smile, she lifted a glass of water to her mouth and sipped, but the camouflage backfired. Her hands trembled so badly that she spilled water down the front of her blouse. In a sudden and uncontrollable burst of anger, she threw the glass across the room.

"You've ruined me, you bastard," she accused, holding up her trembling hands. "My hands won't stop shaking!"

"The effect on the nervous system will wear away," Karl said, frowning in genuine concern.

"If it doesn't, I'll strangle you some night in your sleep, shaking hands or not!"

"You don't mean that."

"Don't I?"

"I've treated you well, haven't I?"

"Well?" Florence sneered. "You torture me and rape me and then give me food to eat and a place to sleep in between rapes, and you call that treating someone well?"

Karl opened his mouth to reply and then closed it, speechless.

Florence rose from her chair and stalked over to the sleeping section. She stretched out on the blankets with her back toward Karl.

She formed a mental list of the ways he had hurt her: 1) The humiliation of being forced to go nude before a group of men; 2) Shot by arrows, one in the leg, one in the arm; 3) Burned her breast with a branding iron; 4)Tortured by a Zeanorian ray gun; 5) Raped.

She knew that Karl loved her, and from all appearances it was much more than a physical desire for her body. But nevertheless, she would make him pay for those five items!

24

When the medical staff at the Aerie decided their health was well enough for Alicia and Eric to sleep together again, something had changed deep inside Eric. New doors had been opened. Vita had taken him to a Zeanorian spaceship deep in the desert and explained they were very close to making it operational again.

"We've been working on it for years," Vita said. "The parts have been perfectly preserved in this dry environment. No one from Homebase or the tribes has been able to travel this far across the desert, and no one other than ourselves has known about it. But some parts of the system were damaged. We've been fitting pieces of the ships together so we can build one operational ship to take us back to the stars. I think the ship you discovered in the jungle may have the remaining parts we need."

The idea of having a ship that could once more

journey through outer space intrigued him to the point of obsession. Vita said she wanted him to be on the crew that journeyed into space again, and he began dreaming of finding new worlds in other galaxies.

In addition to that tremendous distraction, Vita began teaching him the operation of the Zeanorian antigravity belts. They flew together in the clouds, side by side. They drifted on warm winds and landed on the edges of cliffs, resting, gazing down at the ground thousands of feet below, like two eagles at rest before their next flight. Something unexplainable began happening inside Eric, something he could not put into words or fully comprehend. He began feeling a strong emotional involvement with Vita. He desired her sexually but this other feeling was strange and more powerful. He felt it whenever he looked at her, and especially in moments when they were high above the clouds, drifting along with the sun and wind, she holding his hand as they flew together, turning to look at him and smile.

Sometimes he felt torn apart by the dazzling new elements in his life. Sheila and he arranged to meet three or four times a week, their encounters secret and brief, but sexually explosive. He knew it was what their ancestors in the old civilization on earth called an affair. He knew there were certain dangers, but he found Sheila irresistible.

His feelings toward Alicia changed and dwindled beneath the pressure of the three new elements in his life. One day, after he finished telling Alicia how Vita had been instructing him in the use of the

Zeanorian flying belt, Alicia began crying. When he tried to comfort her and asked what was wrong, she refused to answer at first, and then her thoughts and fears flowed like a burst dam:

"Can't you see it? She's seducing you. She could have chosen someone else to teach you how to use the antigravity belt, but she wanted to be with you more often. You should see the expression on your face when you talk about Vita and how you fly above the clouds with her and perch on mountain tops. You love it. She sensed you would love flying. She's filling your head with dreams of traveling to other worlds in one of the Zeanorian starships. You're falling in love with her. I'm losing your love because she's taking it away from me. She wants to take you with them when the ship goes to the stars again. But there isn't any talk of my going, is there? She wants to leave me behind!

"Who is the other woman in your life, Eric? Do you think I'm stupid or blind or both? Almost every day you sneak off somewhere and meet someone. I know it's not Vita because I've been with her-sometimes when you've disappeared. And then you come back from this other woman with a sheepish grin on your face and dragging your feet like she's really—"

She fumbled mentally for the right words, could not find them, and finished angrily, "I wish I was back in the towers! Everything has changed! Nothing is the way you said it would be! I've been asking questions and the women here have what they call dormitories. There's one dormitory where they're very friendly and said they'd like to have me live with them.'' She rose suddenly, standing with her hands on her hips, glaring down at him. "And I think I want to do it! You hardly ever make love to me anymore. When you do, you act like it's an obligation. I'm losing you to two other women and dreams of traveling to other worlds! I think I'm going to leave you, Eric! You big, dumb dummy!''

And, tears streaming down her cheeks, she spun around and almost ran from the room.

Eric sat in stunned silence. Alicia had become his wife according to the old traditions on earth. But he realized now that he had been flying in more than one way than with Vita in the clouds. He had the excitement of sex with Sheila, the newness of falling in love with Vita, and the exotic anticipation of soon traveling to other worlds in other galaxies.

But there was an ancient phrase for this other new element in his life:

His wife had left him.

25

The lights were low in the room and the alien music came through the semidarkness with a strange impact. It was a party to celebrate Alicia's joining their group. It was a party unlike any party Alicia had ever attended.

Two couples of girls were dancing in the shadows. Others were highly intoxicated through one means or another. Some fully clothed, some partially clothed, others completely nude. As the alien music began to seep its way into her mood, Alicia was uncomfortably aware that several of the girls were joined together in one corner, their bodies entwined.

"Work hard, play hard," one of the girls nearby muttered drunkenly to Alicia. "Eat, drink, and be merry, for tomorrow may be as dull as the proverbial dishwater."

One of the girls was friendlier than any of the

others, although Alicia could not remember her name. Moving closer, her new friend extended her hand and Alicia saw a pill on the outstretched palm. "Take one," she coaxed. "It'll make you feel better. You're too uptight."

Alicia stared at the pill. "What is it?"

"We call it a happy pill."

The pills had been banned from Homebase many years ago but this subcolony was beyond the main colony's control. She remembered the stories about such pills, how they could become so addictive the user would soon want them more than anything else.

"You'll feel better afterwards," her friend urged.

Alicia hesitated and said, "No. Thank you, anyway."

"We're not asking you to take a dozen. Just one to get you high for the party in your honor."

She had been thinking of Eric, maybe losing him forever, and feeling close to tears. I need something, she thought. Wouldn't I feel stupid if I started crying? Tonight. Only tonight.

She took the pill and swallowed it.

They had been giving her one pill after another and Alicia had started to take them greedily. She was getting higher and higher. Everything was wonderful and would be wonderful forever and ever.

A young girl made love to her and her friend sat nearby, watching, commenting afterwards, "You don't need Eric. You'll never need Eric again."

165

Her mind soared and her flesh felt numb. She felt as if she could fly physically, but continually stumbled when she tried to walk. She wanted to go into long speeches to tell everyone how much she enjoyed their friendship but the words were garbled when she opened her mouth. The music from another civilization beat a rhythm on her nervous system.

Then she and her new companion were moving down a long, dark corridor. She could not remember where they were going or why. At the end of the corridor they stepped into an exotic room that gave the sensation of stepping into another room on a different planet. There were partitions of shimmering energy, more of the alien music, and a man chained to the floor.

"This is one of our prisoners," her companion explained. "We have nine altogether. We keep them hungry." She laughed and said, "I'll show you why." Reaching up to a shelf on the wall, she withdrew a jar and handed it to Alicia. "Our prisoners love this honey. We hold back on their food so they're always half starved, and when we feed them we give them bland foods, so they go wild when they get a chance to taste this. I'll show you how it works." She smeared some of the honey on her toes and the prisoner greedily licked it away. She applied more honey to the calf of a leg and then spread some on the inside of her thigh. Alicia watched with mounting excitement as the captive licked the honey into his hungry mouth.

The girl said, "I'll leave you two alone so you can amuse yourselves." She gave the jar to Alicia.

"Why is he a prisoner?" Alicia whispered as she followed the other to the doorway.

"He killed one of our members. Raped her and killed her. He was given a fair trial and sentenced to death. His appointed lawyer had his sentence commuted. He was given this alternative, and he selected this rather than dying."

As in a dream, Alicia found herself alone with the prisoner and spreading honey on her toes. It tickled when he obediently licked the honey like a well-trained animal. She spread honey higher and higher on her legs. Because he was chained so he could move only his head and shoulders, she had to shift her position occasionally. Her excitement grew as he ate the honey from her thighs . . . higher . . . higher . . .

She could not remember returning to the dormitory. She was suddenly there, flat on her back, staring at the ceiling where an alien kaleidoscope flickered soothingly, summoning her mind towards sleep. A voice said softly, "How did you like it?"

Her new friend was kneeling by her cot, her face in shadows. All the other girls were asleep.

"Wonderful," Alicia admitted.

"There are all kinds of fringe benefits to being in a subcolony where the main purpose is studying the relics of another civilization."

"I'm starting to realize that," Alicia said, glancing up at the gentle kaleidoscope on the ceiling. She knew the hypnotic effect would soon draw her into a sound and restful sleep whenever she wanted.

"We have benefits and comforts that even the Guiders and Techs at Homebase do not have—all because we learned how to convert the Zeanorian machines to our own needs."

"Homebase was never this comfortable or interesting or exciting," Alicia agreed.

"So you enjoyed the prisoner?"

Alicia giggled. "I think I had five or six orgasms. They happened so fast I couldn't count them."

"I'm glad you enjoyed yourself."

Something slipped in Alicia's mind. She knew her new friend had been trying to show her all the pleasures available at the Aerie, but something slipped and she abruptly remembered all the times she had been with Eric and how satisfying it had felt to hold him in her arms.

"I want to stay here with everyone else," she blurted, "but I want Eric again." As if the drugs had removed all inhibitions, she confided freely, "He's been making love with another woman. I know. I don't know who she is and maybe that doesn't matter, but there must be something I can do to take him away from her, to make him stop thinking of her, stop wanting her." She was silent awhile, then added, "There must be some way to—to fight for him."

Her new friend did not answer immediately, then responded, "I suppose so. Meanwhile, to keep your mind off your personal problems, would you like to learn how to fly? I could give you lessons starting tomorrow after the work period."

"Oh, that would be wonderful. You've been such a good friend. I'm sorry, I heard so many new

names today I don't remember your name."
"Sheila."

26

Eric drank too much during the visit with the Tree Father. His mind was in that precariously balanced position where he could still think fairly clearly yet knew he had consumed too much.

I haven't done this since the time with Ollie, he thought idly.

The visit with the Tree Father was far from Eric's expectations. Vita and the Elderly man talked about the revolution, the Zeanorian spaceships, travel to another galaxy, and colonization of another world. It seemed as if centuries had passed since Eric had last seen the Tree Father. As he sat and listened to Vita and the old man, his thoughts drifted back to how his life had been. For the majority of his lifetime, everything had seemed so simple. Hazardous but simple. He had been a Hunter. He had learned how to hunt and kill tigers and stay alive.

A Hunter's life is so simple, he thought drunkenly. Eat, sleep, kill. Eat, sleep, kill.

Now there were many complex things filling his life, complex elements he could not fully understand—and some he could not even partially understand. Vita said he had a good mind but he didn't feel that way. Recently he had felt stupid and confused most of the time.

He drank some more and realized how much he missed Alicia.

I risked my life for her, he thought bitterly.

The thing with Sheila. It had seemed beyond his control. As he continued to drink, it amazed him that he had been so powerless over the involvement. He had fought men and tigers and won. But Sheila had always been in command of their relationship. He had found himself unable to resist her. Alicia had been jealous of Vita for no reason, he thought. He liked Vita and was attracted toward her—she was a fascinating woman—but they had not become sexually involved. Sometimes he wondered if their relationship would go beyond the boundaries of platonic friendship.

Ironic, he thought. Here I am, involved in a revolution and the preparations for intergalactic travel, and my main concern is the women in my life.

He wondered drunkenly if men had always been that way. Perhaps the first space travelers had been more concerned about their love life than the mechanics of the starships.

He wandered outside, bought a fresh bottle from one of the old men who lived near the Tree Father, and continued to drink until thinking became almost impossible.

171

At one point he found Vita standing nearby, hands on hips, looking down at him accusingly.

"Eric, the Brave, great Hunter. Hiding in a bottle, drunk. Hiding from life, Eric?" And then, before he had a chance to ask her what she meant by the remark about hiding in a bottle, she turned and went away.

At another point when he was alone with the Tree Father, almost in tears, he complained to the Father that nothing had gone as he had planned and that he couldn't understand nine-tenths of the things that had happened in his life recently. With his usual patience, the Father explained that many men resolved such things by acceptance of what some called the Highest Power.

The Highest Power, the father explained, often manipulated, changed, and directed events according to His own masterplan. "And, as mere men," the Tree Father summed, "we cannot fully understand His majestic schemes. When we are fortunate we are able to comprehend on an infinitesimal fragment of His infinite design."

Eric nodded agreement. It sounded right, but at the moment he was having difficulty understanding anything. Vita appeared and announced they should return to the Aerie before dark.

27

As the lessons in the use of the Zeanorian antigravity belt began, Alicia felt a mixture of pleasant anticipation and apprehension. The idea of being able to fly as high as the clouds seemed wonderful. But she knew there would be dangers, especially the one of falling a great height. Mingled with that apprehension was a confused feeling toward her instructor Sheila. Sheila had been her closest friend at the Aerie, but now she acted strangely, as if she no longer liked Alicia.

The preliminary instructions were relatively easy to understand. But then, as they lifted away from the mesa, hovered a hundred feet above the mesa top and began to move toward a distant mountain range, Alicia found it increasingly difficult to follow Sheila's instructions. She did not fully understand how to compensate for wind velocity. While on a supposedly level and straight flight toward a distant mountain pass, she found herself drifting first to one side and then to the other as she either overcompensated or undercompensated for the wind.

Passing through the mountain range, they encountered vicious downdrafts and updrafts. Again Alicia had difficulty understanding Sheila's instructions. At times it seemed that Sheila was deliberately misleading her for some strange reason.

The mountain pass became narrower and narrower, simultaneously curving first in one direction and then another. Sheila was able to maintain a constant level and equal distance from each cliff face. Alicia, however, found herself unable to compensate for the updrafts and downdrafts. At first she would be higher than Sheila, then lower.

She's giving me too much to learn too fast, Alicia thought desperately. But what could she do except struggle to learn?

As they proceeded through the mountain pass, Alicia came dangerously close to the cliff faces several times.

We're going too fast, she realized. Sheila shouldn't be traveling this fast with someone learning the antigravity belt operation. She wants me to be hurt or killed!

Moments after the realization, she had her first accident. A startling updraft flipped her and turned her to one side before she could compensate. Her head struck a slab of rock and she blacked out. When she regained consciousness she was falling toward a canyon river far below. She maneuvered the controls to stop her descent and felt the wetness of

174

blood trickling down one cheek from a gash in her skull.

A sudden gust of wind slammed her against a ragged cliff. She felt the flesh on her left hip tear as if struck and ripped by several knives. As she managed to pull away from the cliff, she now felt blood trickling down her left leg. Somehow she managed to continue on for a few hundred yards and—suddenly—another updraft spun her wildly until her right shoulder slammed against a rock. This time she did not feel the moisture of blood but her whole right arm and hand felt numb.

Using her right hand on the controls was impossible. Moving her left hand to the control buttons and knobs, she struggled to rise from the canyon and escape the dangers of updrafts and downdrafts by climbing above the mountains altogether. She turned and looked in every direction.

Sheila had disappeared.

She left me to die, Alicia thought bitterly. She brought me to this trap of a canyon and hoped I would be hurt or killed.

Alicia managed to climb hundreds of feet above the mountain range and felt a new blackness closing in.

When she regained consciousness, she found the antigravity belt had carried her thousands of feet above a layer of clouds. She looked down upon a billowy field of white and was amazed that she was still alive. She felt faint and weak and cold from the loss of blood. Her right arm still felt numb. Her lungs were laboring in the thin air.

Fumbling with the belt controls, she descended

through the clouds and—

Descended into the boiling nightmare of an electrical storm.

As the irresistible currents turned her first one way and then the other, she lost all sense of direction. The lightning frightened her at first as it traveled what seemed only yards away. Then, as she felt weaker and weaker, she began hoping that a bolt of lightning would strike and kill her instantly.

I'm going to die, she thought with a sick feeling inside. Sheila wanted to kill me for some reason. She planned how to do it and then left me to struggle on my own.

Even if she survived the storm, she would be alone, lost, miles from the mesa. Weak from loss of blood and shock, she could easily lose consciousness and control of the antigravity belt. It would be so easy to fall thousands of feet while unconscious and strike the ground with all the force of a falling rock.

If I don't die by falling, she thought, I could die from starvation. I could be so lost I wouldn't be able to find either the mesa or Homebase.

I'm going to die, she thought in panic. One way or another, I will die!

Resigned to her death, she thought, Eric, Eric, Eric, and slipped into another deep darkness.

28

The revolution was winding down and many months had passed since the disappearance of Alicia.

Halfway toward Homebase on the assigned reconnaissance flight, Sheila found a position in a valley of clouds and adjusted the flying belt so all momentum ceased. She removed her clothes, tied them into a small bundle, and suspended it at the end of her necklace which she in turn fastened to a link of the Zeanorian antigravity belt.

Once nude she turned onto her back and studied her surroundings. A white wall of clouds towered high on one side and sloped gently upward on the other three sides. She was hidden from the ground on all sides. Only someone passing overhead could see her, and the odds were against that. Only one other person should be in the air at this vicinity and that was Vita.

If her calculations were correct, Vita should be moving toward the Aerie now, a mile or two away, having completed her segment of the reconnaisance.

This is perfect, she thought, a perfect place to sunbathe.

She drifted with the wind in her private valley of clouds, luxuriating in the warmth of the sun.

I'll have the best tan at the Aerie, she gloated. Eric loves my dark, tanned body. I'll make it even darker for him.

Eyes closed, she began thinking how everything had changed since Alicia's disappearance long ago.

There had been suspicions, of course. There had been dozens and dozens of questions. Sheila had stuck to her story that a storm had caught and separated them. She did not know for certain that Alicia had been killed. A search party had failed to find her body.

After the efforts of the search proved fruitless, everyone had grown cooler toward her. Alicia had been well liked and everyone acted as if they blamed Sheila.

Sex with Eric had ceased. This was the greatest physical change in her life. Eric had aroused her more than any other man. He had stirred her to heights of excitement she would have thought impossible. She had decided to kill Alicia to avoid losing him. Ironically she had lost Eric because of Alicia's death. Eric had mourned Alicia's disappearance and lost all interest in sex. Temporarily, Sheila knew.

They were getting very close to reaching their goal

of making a Zeanorian starship operable again. Vita and Eric had been traveling to the alien ship he had discovered in the jungle. They'd been removing one component after another and installing them in the amalgamated desert ship. Everyone said they had to only transfer two or three more components and the starship would be completely operable. The anticipation of returning to the stars again had been growing, spreading through the subcolony with the flavor of an exotic dream.

Sheila turned on her stomach, floating in the air, gazing down at the billowy white floor of her private valley with eyes half-closed as the rays of sun warmed her back. The three elements—coolness of her associates since Alicia's death, Eric's withdrawal, and the anticipation of intergalactic travel—had changed everything in her life.

And her own attitude had changed. At first she had been actively interested in the revolution. She had taken these recon flights over Homebase seriously, trying to observe the Guiders and discern their defenses and tactics. Recently, however, it had all started to seem like childish war games and she spent most of the last four recon flights sunbathing in the clouds.

When the sun began to burn her back slightly and when she found herself becoming sweaty, she decided to descend beneath the clouds to see if she could find a rainfall in the vicinity. Twice before she had used such a rainfall as a colossal and exhiliarating shower in the sky.

When she touched the controls to descend, she heard a distinct click within the mechanism and it began lifting her rather than descending.

She touched the other controls, her fingers flying over the buttons and levers.

Nothing happened. She continued to rise.

How could the antigravity belt malfunction? she wondered.

She was rising higher and higher above the clouds. She had no tools to take the belt apart, nothing except her bare fingers.

Higher and higher.

The air became thin and chilly. As she shivered in the cold air and gasped for breath, she wondered if someone had tampered with the flying belt to kill her.

Nothing worked. Nothing could stop the belt from carrying her into the stratosphere.

I'll die, she thought.

Nearly unconscious, a desperate plan formed in her mind.

The only method that might work.

She turned the belt off. She began to fall.

When Sheila turned the antigravity belt on again, the jolt was so strong that she lost consciousness. She regained consciousness several minutes later and found the belt once more carrying her toward the stratosphere.

I was lucky I didn't kill myself, she thought. I'll have to be more careful . . . not make the drops so long. How shall I work it? Turn the belt off and count to twenty? Then turn the belt on only an instant to break the fall? And this way lower myself?

She turned the belt off and counted to twenty.

Heart pounding with nervousness, she touched

the belt control lever. Suppose it doesn't work? Her mind screamed. I'll fall thousands of feet and be crushed by the impact. She turned the belt on and felt a jolt as the antigravity belt stopped her fall.

She repeated the process of turning the belt off, falling, counting to twenty, and turning it back on, beginning the ascent again but never as high as before.

She tried counts of ten and fifteen to lessen the stress to her body, but the lower count made the descent seem endless, and she went back to the count of twenty.

Like jumping down from the sky in steps, she thought wildly. If I can get down from the sky, I can survive anything else.

Descending through the clouds, she once more thought, Did someone tamper with the antigravity belt?

Questions after Alicia's disappearance had been endless. No one had seen her with Eric, but a few people had seen Eric and her together shortly before and after love making. So. Someone must have certainly put two and two together. And after Alicia's disappearance, someone could have accurately assumed that she had eliminated Alicia for her own personal reasons. And, therefore, someone could have tampered with her antigravity belt to eliminate her.

She was falling from the clouds now, the earth still far below.

It wouldn't be safe to return to the Aerie even if I could manage it somehow, she thought. The someone would be certain to make a second attempt on my life.

The ocean appeared beneath the clouds, totally surprising her. In a sudden panic she realized, the strong winds at the higher altitudes had carried her hundreds of miles.

With a sensation of complete hopelessness, she knew she was trapped. If she turned off the antigravity belt and fell into the ocean, she would drown. If she tried to stay in the air with the faulty antigravity belt, it would kill her in one way or another, either by jolting her body to death or else carrying her into the stratosphere where she would either freeze to death or suffocate in the thin air.

All her life she had coped with problems, difficulties, and hazards. Now, for the first time, with a feeling of total hopelessness, she knew she was lost.

29

Nurse Fay and Guider Falcon had made their decision in stages. Somewhere in the long talks, they decided that Johnny could be their son. The could had changed to a positive attitude in which they both agreed it would be best for their emotional health if they assumed Johnny was theirs.

The desire to be free of the restrictions of Homebase had grown. Everyone felt certain that Homebase would be attacked in the near future and the impending danger to the children became more and more apparent. Plans were being made to evacuate the children and some adults into the mountains where small subcolonies would be formed.

And this was the point at which Nurse Fay suggested they take Johnny and join the Tree People. It would be easy, she said, during his portion of guard duty at the perimeter for the three of them to simply walk away.

"That would be desertion," Guider Falcon argued.

"Desertion from what?" Nurse Fay countered. "There is no political party involved, no country such as our ancestors owed their allegiance to. We're nothing more than groups of people who started a colony on another world and found ourselves living in this place or that place. Desertion isn't the right word. We'd simply be deciding where we want to live."

Falcon was hesitant to follow Nurse Fay's suggestion. As the days passed the need to evacuate the children into small subcolonies in the mountains became more and more obvious.

"That will drag the revolution on forever," Nurse Fay insisted. "The Outsiders will hold back from attacking the subcolonies for fear of hurting innocent children. The adults with each group will use the children as shields to strike back at the Outsiders. Can you imagine how horrible that environment would be? The combination of fear and hate?"

The next evening, Falcon was in a position as one of the perimeter observers. He had tried unsuccessfully to shove thoughts of Nurse Fay and Johnny from his mind. His deepest emotions were in a turmoil. The structures of Homebase loomed in the shadows on one side, dark shapes spotted with lights. Voices drifted on a faint breeze. Human voices mingled with the strange sound of Zeanorian music. This is a bizarre way of life, he thought. Stranded on an alien world with the remnants of another race that was also not native to this world.

184

Nurse Fay appeared silently in the shadows, holding Johnny's hand. A dozen thoughts rushed through Falcon's mind. This was her way of forcing the issue. If the three of them left, it would kick off other desertions. So far there had been a mutual trust among everyone at Homebase. In the future that trust would be shaken.

He wanted to go but couldn't. The muscles in his legs refused to move. Fay was looking at him and he knew she was struggling to keep her face as expressionless as possible. When he did not respond in any way, she moved past him toward the forest.

Fay and Johnny were several yards away when they stopped suddenly.

Two glowing eyes were directly before them in the shadows. They did not know if the creature was harmless or not. Falcon realized that Nurse Fay had not thought to bring a weapon of any sort, that they might have to travel miles in the dark forest before they encountered an Outsider.

He found himself running to join them, eager to explain that the eyes in the shadows were harmless, only a type of owl that used its luminous eyes to attract insects which it would hastily devour. But there were other strange animals in the forest he would have to protect them from, and he knew he would go with them not because he wanted to be a part of the new society that struggled for life, but because he wanted to be with her and Johnny no matter where they went.

Florence lay with her back toward the tent entrance, waiting. She knew Karl would be returning any minute, and she wanted to fake sleep, force him to make the first overtures this evening.

News of the attack on Homebase had preceded Karl's return. She had been proud to hear that he had launched a successful attack with a minimum of casualties to either side. Homebase had been conquered and was now being occupied by the revolutionists. Handfuls of Guiders and Techs were supposedly hiding in the mountains, but it was generally considered that the revolution was over. Karl had launched the Archers against Homebase defenses in some brilliant maneuvers. The Techs and Guiders had expected the Archers to attack with only bows and arrows, but Karl had employed several Zeanorian weapons, and the attack, with the help of an alien technology, had thoroughly unnerved the defenders. Hearing the excited news, she thought, I'm proud of my man. She realized immediately afterward that she had been thinking of Karl as her man for several days. She could not recall exactly how and when she had assumed the role of proprietor.

She heard Karl undressing and bathing. He slipped into fresh clothing. Then a long silence followed in which she guessed he must be sitting and watching her silent back. She wondered what thoughts were going through his mind. She felt almost guilty. She had used every womanly trick to get him under her control.

"Flo?" He touched her shoulder gently.

She yawned, rolled on her side to face him, smiled with feigned sleepiness. The expression on his face was marvelous. He was bursting with pride to tell her the revolution had ended. Won. And she felt pride, too. Karl had confided to her that a specialized team of workers had been preparing a Zeanorian starship for its first intergalactic flight in centuries. He had been selected as one of the crew members and expeditionary force. He was, she thought, quite a man. Capable of conquering a city or a planet or a galaxy.

30

A short distance beyond the main entrance to the spaceship, Vita removed an access panel and uncovered the inlet to a long, narrow, dark passageway.

"You carry the light," Vita directed. "I'll carry the computer and tools."

They had to crawl on their hands and knees. Eric reflected on the number of times he'd passed the access panel without the slightest idea it was a doorway, seeing it only as a rectangular design in the wall at that point. He had used the ship as a halfway base for quite awhile, used it for storage of tiger skins and spears long before he met Alicia and brought her there.

Thoughts of Alicia once more brought the familiar pain of loss. It had been months since she had vanished, and only recently had he reluctantly assumed that she must be dead. The pain was less each time the memories returned. Vita and the others had conspired to fill his time with a maze of activities, and his mind with a multitude of concepts and projects. During the past weeks Vita had involved him in the reconstruction of what most called their amalgamated ship. Some called it *Amalthaea*. Amalthaea was the name of the nurse of Zeus, described as a goat, and one whose horn magically filled with whatever its possessor wished. This horn was known as the horn of cornucopia, the horn of plenty. A fitting name for the ship, Eric thought.

At the end of the tunnel the passageway narrowed.

"We'll have to squirm on our stomachs the last three yards," Vita informed him. "And then we'll find ourselves in a small compartment where we'll at least be able to sit."

"Is that what the ship diagrams show?" Eric asked doubtfully.

"All the Zeanorian ships are identical," Vita reminded him. "I've gone through this same passageway in the other starships."

After Eric heard the answer, he felt stupid for having asked. They squirmed through the narrower section of the passageway. He experienced some claustrophobia as the walls became so tight that they squeezed his shoulders. Then they were through and into the compartment Vita had mentioned.

"This is what we call a maintenance cubicle," Vita started to explain. "It—"

The words froze in her throat as they saw the cubicle was already occupied.

He had been dead for a long time. Eric stared at

the skeleton of the Zeanorian and realized it was in much better condition than any of the other skeletons he'd found in the ship. Its uniform was gray with age but still intact.

"That's the uniform of the starship maintenance engineers," Vita said. "I wonder . . . As far as we can reconstruct the events, something happened to all the Zeanorian starships simultaneously. They were forced to land here. So far we haven't been able to determine what went wrong in their ship systems. After they landed, something either malfunctioned with their life support system or else they died from some sort of disease. The question we've never been able to find the answer to is whether or not they contracted the disease before they landed or after. Maybe the answer isn't important . . . But see, there's a tool in the skeleton's hand, and a set of other tools by his side. He crawled in here to make some repairs. I wonder—" Eric was watching her changes of expression as she mused and then bit her lower lip thoughtfully. She went on, "Could it be he guessed what the trouble was and came here to repair it?"

She turned to look at Eric with blank eyes as she pondered then answered her own question. "That's possible. The next question would be, Did he succeed in making the repairs before he died?"

Vita began working with the probes, portable power supply, and computer. Eric remembered that Vita once explained that the Zeanorian starship units were designed so each unit served several purposes. This facet of the ships design had been useful to the Zeanorians so they could shut down a unit for repairs or maintenance while the particular functions involved were routed through other multipurpose units. Vita had explained that the system had also allowed the Zeanorians to change, improve, and adapt their spaceships while in flight.

This was the last component needed to make *Amalthaea* operable again. According to the engineers in charge, this unit, one that handled phases of the spacewarp drive, galactic navigation, and life support system, was a final link that would make a test flight possible—and eventually bring intergalactic travel once more within their grasp.

Eric held the light as Vita worked. She moved the probes from place to place, injecting surges of power here and punching questions into the small computer there. He expected the testing to take only a few minutes but it went on for hours. Vita seemed oblivious of time, deep in concentration, feeding more and more into the computer. Eric began to fully appreciate the importance of the testing of this component. This was the culmination of decades of work. Failure or success grew closer and closer.

Vita groaned. At first Eric thought it was a groan of failure and dismay. An instant later he knew it was a cry of deep joy. Success. The last component needed to put *Amalthaea* into the stars was in place. Vita embraced him. They kissed. She seemed mindless with joy and Eric began to absorb the mood.

Eric remembered what the Tree Father had said, and for one startling moment he felt he could comprehend a fragment of the Highest Power's cosmic design. He could not understand the functions of the Zeanorian starship, but it would soon take them to the stars again.

Vita interrupted his thoughts, suddenly gasping with pleasure and satisfaction, then whispered, "We are free again, Eric. Free to travel to the stars!"